I0554531

Ryder's Redemption

BOOKS BY J.A. TEMPLETON

Available in Print and eBook

The MacKinnon Curse series
(Mature YA Paranormal Romance)
THE DEEPEST CUT
THE HAUNTED
THE DEPARTED
THE MACKINNON CURSE (Novella)

COMING SOON:
THE GATEKEEPER
The Immortals of Parthas series
(New Adult Fantasy Romance)

Ryder's Redemption by J.A. Templeton

Copyright 2014 Julia Templeton
Print ISBN: 978-1-939863-07-2
eBook ISBN: 978-1-939863-04-1

Printed in the USA

This book is a work of fiction. Characters and events portrayed in this book are products of the writer's imagination or have been used fictitiously and are not to be construed as real. Any resemblance to persons, living or dead, or actual events is entirely coincidental and not intended by the author.

All rights reserved. No part of this book may be reproduced, scanned, or distributed in any manner whatsoever without written permission from the author.

Cover Photograph by Korie Nicole Photography
Cover Illustration by MaeIDesign
Editing by The Passionate Proofreader
Interia Design by Lasting Impressions eBook Creations

Ryder's Redemption

A Thin White Line Novel

J. A. Templeton

Printed in the USA

To Steven (Steve) Joseph—

For being the best big brother-in-law a girl could ask for. You're the toughest guy I know, and yet one of the kindest, especially when it comes to your brother. Thanks for loving him and always being there for him. The unbreakable bond you two share is inspiring.

Author note: Steve died during the writing of this novel. The character of Uncle Steve was loosely based on Steve, and more importantly, the relationship between Steve and my husband, Kip was the inspiration for Ryder and Deklan's relationship. Steve and Kip were "soul" brothers and their relationship was absolutely beautiful. Kip and Steve never parted ways before giving each other a big hug and telling each other "I love you." Steve was the kind of guy you would want in your corner. Fiercely loyal, incredibly compassionate, a complete badass when he had to be, and a source of comfort like no other when times were tough.

Steve, this one's for you—for being one of my biggest supporters and a dear friend, for being such a wonderful uncle to my children, and mostly for being an incredible brother to my husband who adored you.
I will see you on the other side, my friend!

We love and miss you...

ONE

R^{yder}

My fingernails bite into the armrest.

All around me, I hear the sound of buzzing tattoo guns. I concentrate on a black-and-white photograph of a Louisiana cemetery that is carefully positioned, along with a dozen other photographs, on the dark red walls of *Branded*, the tattoo parlor where my best friend Deklan works. The shop's owner, Uncle Steve, is one twisted motherfucker. I find myself wondering why he's so intrigued by death. Even the glass case at the front of the shop holds shelves of antique medical devices and other oddities, including a shrunken head that he swears is originally from Ecuador. Apparently he has the paperwork to prove it.

Not that anyone would want to question Uncle Steve. He's the most intimidating guy on the planet. Bald, goateed, with badass tattoos, many from his prison days, Uncle

Steve's demeanor screams "don't mess with me." I know he struggled with his own addictions in his time. Cost him a marriage, custody of his two kids, and a decade and then some in one of the roughest Federal penitentiaries in the U.S.. I never asked what for. In fact, I was a little terrified to know the truth.

I was just grateful he had opened a place like *Branded* for us to come to, and where my best buddy, a guy I considered my brother, could showcase his talent. Like Uncle Steve, Deklan was one of the best tattoo artists in the county.

"Dude, you're sweating."

I glance up at my best friend. Deklan is grinning from ear to ear, looking a little too happy to be the one giving me my first tattoo. I'm not regretting the Celtic trinity knot that he's presently carving into my upper right arm. I just wish I had gone with something that had less definition. "It's not too bad," I say, even as my nails dug deeper into the leather. In a way, I welcomed the pain. I haven't used for six days, five hours, and—I glance at the clock—twenty-six minutes. Without a doubt, this week has been the longest of my life.

For some reason since quitting drugs, I've become obsessed with time. Thinking that somehow, by watching the clock, the days will go by faster. Each day I try to find the joy out of each endless second, but I'm fucking miserable.

Honestly, I didn't realize how addicted to painkillers I've become. How I've thrived on being numb and not feeling my life.

For four years now, I've been using some kind of substance—whether it be alcohol, prescription drugs, illegal drugs. You name it…I've used it. And it's not like I didn't function during that time. I pulled decent grades, was always punctual, and made it to practice with my band without ever missing a beat.

Unbelievable. Here I thought I was in control and that I would never be ruled by emotions or my habits.

Some habits died hard, and I was struggling.

Big time.

The buzzer at the front door went off and Deklan lifted his head. I'm immediately relieved by the short break. That is, until I see his eyes light up. I know who the new arrival is without looking.

Kenzie…also known as my biggest mistake.

If I hadn't been such a cheating prick, she would still be my girl, not Deklan's.

Kenzie is everything I'm not. Sweet, light, and good.

I am well aware that chicks like Kenzie come around just once in a lifetime, and I'm reminded of that every single time I see her gorgeous face. She's the quintessential California babe. Sun-kissed golden skin, natural blonde hair with highlights, minimal makeup that made it look like she'd just rolled out of bed. And her eyes—God, she has killer eyes. Blue eyes, the irises like tiny flower petals. In a word, she was unique.

"Hey babe." She runs her fingers through Deklan's dark hair, bends down, and gives him a soft welcoming kiss.

Deklan smiles against her lips, and I bite down on the inside of my cheek.

Her long golden blonde hair is tied back in a ponytail. Dressed in a white tank, jean shorts, and flip-flops, she draws everyone's eye. She has no idea how gorgeous she is. How men are drawn to her like bees to honey.

The way she's looking at my best friend, with absolute love and adoration in her eyes, makes me wonder how I wasn't able to see it before now. I think back during our concerts and remember seeing her in the crowd, how her eyes would shift from me to Deklan. And afterward, when we all hung out together, the glances they shared had lingered a little. But Deklan and I had never fought over a chick, and I didn't think for a second that the two of them would end up together.

Or that he'd go for her. I trusted him more than I trusted anyone.

And I knew him well enough to know that Kenzie was the one.

My buddy was the happiest I'd ever seen him.

I clear my throat and Kenzie pulls away from Deklan.

"Ryder, you're finally taking the plunge," Kenzie says, her lips curving into a soft smile.

I force a grin. "Yeah, Deklan pressured me."

Deklan frowns in my direction. "I didn't force you to sit here."

"You've been on my ass for years about getting inked."

"You finally grew a pair is what happened," Deklan murmurs under his breath, a smile playing at the corners of his mouth.

I'd wanted a tattoo forever, but my mom forbade me to get one while I lived under her roof. Truth be told, that's the main reason I'm getting inked now—I want to piss her off.

Just thinking about my mom makes my blood boil. She'd always made a point to let everyone know her opinion, regardless if you asked for it or not. Everyone was entitled to her opinion, or so she said. She would disown me the second she found out about the tattoo. All my life she'd had a set of guidelines—rules of the household. I loved my mom. She was the cool and calculated wife, President of the PTA, stay-at-home mom, Sunday school teacher. She dressed impeccably, acted impeccably, and expected her family to do the same. She was a pillar of the community. However, she wasn't always the uptight bitch that she was today. I vaguely remember the mom who wore jeans, tennis shoes, and sweatshirts, the one who hadn't been afraid to get her hands dirty. That mom had gone away with my father's success.

Deklan had been an experiment of sorts for her. Everyone praised her for her generosity in taking in the son of drug addicts. My mom had always liked Deklan. What wasn't to like? He had gone out of his way to please her. Having never had a mom and dad who were any good at parenting or gave two shits about him, Deklan had fully embraced my parents and my structured existence. I'd loved it, too, because Deklan had an incredible work ethic, and that hadn't changed from the time he was a kid. He couldn't sit still without feeling like he should be doing something productive, he'd once told me, and so he took care of his chores and mine too.

He just made life easier for me all the way around.

Needless to say, Deklan never disappointed my mom. Nor had my twelve year-old brother. No, I was my mom's biggest disappointment, and she had made that clear when I had told her I had a drug problem and needed help. Her way of helping was showing me the door and telling me not to come back until I could piss clean. Literally, those were her words, which had been especially shocking since I rarely heard her cuss.

It had been my turn to ask Deklan for help.

I'd shown up on Deklan's doorstep that night and he'd taken me in with open arms. He'd been my constant companion ever since. And I mean constant.

I know he keeps such a close eye on me because he is terrified I will fall off the wagon.

"Can we continue?" Deklan asks, the tattoo gun coming back to life.

I nod. "What are you up to?" I ask Kenzie, gritting my teeth as the needle bites into my skin.

She pulls up a chair beside Deklan. Her hand lingers on his thigh. Their relationship is easy, natural, and I find myself jealous of it the more I'm around them.

"Ange flies in this afternoon. I pick her up in ninety minutes."

"Ange, as in your California buddy?"

"Yeah, my California buddy." Kenzie is beaming, she's so happy. From what I've heard of this girl, she's as pure as the driven snow. One of Kenzie's all-girl Catholic school classmates. Filthy rich, too.

"How long is she here for?"

"Five weeks."

In a way, I'm relieved her goody two-shoes buddy is arriving. That means there will be five weeks that I'll have Deklan more to myself. At first I didn't really mind being a third wheel, but after a while it's gotten to be a major pain in the ass.

"She's going to check out WSU while she's here," Kenzie says, excitement in her voice. "That way we'll be together again."

"Yeah, Deklan said you were interested in attending college next year." I wink. "Not just a pretty face, huh?"

Deklan lifts his brow, his gaze shifting between Kenzie and me.

She smiles at me, and I hate that my heart skips a beat.

"Dude, you want to take a break?"

"Christ, how long is this tattoo going to take?"

He rubs the tattoo down and smiles at me. "Just messing with you. You're finished."

Thank God. If I ever have another tattoo, I'm taking a few straight shots beforehand.

I slide out of the chair and walk toward the front where Steve's wife, Auntie Phyllis, is ready to pierce a lady's nose. It's obvious the woman has had a tough life. Her hair is listless, her face weathered, teeth dark and fucked up, and the way her foot keeps vibrating against the stool makes me wonder if she's a tweaker.

Phyllis is a pro. She tells the lady to be still unless she wants a hole somewhere other than her nose.

The lady makes a crude response, and it's then she makes eye contact with me.

Her pupils are huge. Slowly, her gaze travels over my body.

Phyllis tracks her gaze and smiles over her shoulder at me. "Put a shirt on, boy, you're distracting the clientele."

I laugh and head out the door, pulling a cigarette from my back pocket.

"Faggot. Put a shirt on," a kid yells from a passing car and I give him the finger.

I light a cigarette and inhale the smoke deep into my lungs. The nicotine instantly calms me. I don't even really like the taste of cigarettes, but it helps take the edge off my aggression and frustration. I promise myself I'll quit once I get a handle on my prescription drug addiction.

Uncle Steve appears from the side of the building. He pulls a smoke out of his flannel shirt chest pocket and lights it.

I have a huge respect for the man, especially since he loves my best friend like his own son…but the dude is scarier than shit. Making and maintaining eye contact is a challenge.

"You struggling?"

I shrug. "I'm alright."

He puts a beefy hand on my shoulder and looks deep into my eyes. "Don't give into it, man. I see the craving in your eyes. I know that feeling."

"I'm six days sober. I'm not going to fuck it up now."

The side of his mouth lifts. "That's what I want to hear."

"I won't let you down." I mean every word, because if I don't follow through, he will probably hunt me down and kill me.

"Don't let my boy in there down." He nods toward Deklan, who is hugging Kenzie. As though he senses my gaze, he glances my way.

"I'll never let him down again."

"If you fuck up, you'll not only have your boy Deklan coming down on you…you'll have me right behind him."

TWO

A ngela

It's been seven months since I've seen my best friend.

A part of me is scared to see Kenzie because she has changed. I could tell from all our conversations since she'd left San Diego that the Kenzie I knew and loved had been hardened by the turn her life had taken since her father had left her mother for a younger woman. Life hadn't been easy for either one of us after she'd left. I'd lost not just my best friend but my constant companion since she walked into Saint Catherine's School for Young Ladies over ten years ago.

We'd immediately clicked and quickly became inseparable. Sometimes I felt she knew me better than I knew myself. I wonder if I would still feel the same way after my trip.

I had expected our friendship to continue as it has been for a while...but I had been stunned when her phone calls started to decline within days of her arrival in Vancouver.

Of course I'd been happy she'd found a friend in her cousin Brooke, and yet I'd been hurt that I'd been replaced so quickly.

Although her phone calls had been fewer than I had hoped for, I had loved those conversations because, in my own way, I had lived vicariously through Kenzie and her rocker clique. She'd explained each person in such detail that I felt I knew them intimately.

And of course I'd searched the band on the Internet. Although not one of the band members had a personal profile online, the band *The Frozen* had a faithful following, and the pictures had validated that Kenzie hadn't lied about how good-looking Deklan and Ryder were.

I could hardly wait to meet Deklan, the man who had swept my best friend off her feet.

But I am more excited to see my girl.

I am both nervous and excited when I finally make my way off the plane. I slide a hand over the skirt of my lace and tulle sundress. Kenzie had been with me when I'd bought it for my seventeenth year birthday celebration, and she'd always said it was one of her favorites.

"Can I get that for you?"

I look over at the middle-aged businessman who has been eyeing me throughout the flight. He's carrying a roll-away suitcase, and he glances at my carry-on.

"No, thank you," I say with a smile.

The man is old enough to be my father, and I freakin' hate the way he's staring at my thighs.

Pig.

"I don't mind", he says, actually reaching for the bag strap. His hand brushes the side of my breast in the process.

I grip the carry-on closer to me and stop short. "No, thank you."

He obviously sees the irritation in my eyes and hears it in my voice because he steps back and walks toward the security posts.

The Portland airport is surprisingly huge, and there is a sea of people waiting for the arriving flights. I smooth a hand over my reddish brown curls and wonder what Kenzie will think of the new highlights.

My heart pounds in time with my steps as I approach the arrival area.

I see him first.

The infamous Deklan.

Tall, dark faux hawk, full sleeve tattoos, piercings—and an athlete's body. He's gorgeous. My stomach actually does a little flip as my gaze slides to my best friend. I suddenly feel overdressed for the occasion. She's wearing faded blue jean shorts, a white tank, and flip-flops. Her long blonde hair is up in a high pony.

Kenzie is stunning. Her blue eyes are full of excitement and she's glowing.

I don't think I'd ever seen her so happy. And I've known her forever. We've shared everything. Every milestone, every hope, every highlight, every sadness, every fear, every celebration.

And lately there has been a lot to celebrate.

She waves at me and actually jumps up and down with excitement.

All my fears that she's replaced me evaporate as I walk past the security barrier and straight into her wide-open arms.

"God, I've missed you," she says, her arms tightening around my neck. It's a hug I feel all the way to my bones and I love it.

"I miss you, too," I manage to squeak out.

She smells the same. Like salon shampoo and that vanilla body spray she's been using since eighth grade.

I notice she's lost weight. Not a lot, but enough for me to tell there is a difference. I can see it in her face, too, but she looks great. She's glowing and I know why.

A lump forms in my throat. I glance up and her boyfriend is watching us, a wide smile on that gorgeous mouth of his. I have to admit the lip piercing is hot and I wonder, for a split second, what it feels like to kiss a guy with a lip ring…or a tongue ring.

The stories she has told me about this smoking hot tattoo artist/rocker makes me blush. She didn't spare a single detail, even the heartache of choosing between best friends and local rock gods who wanted the same girl.

And the best man won.

I'm introduced to Deklan, who surprises me by giving me a breath-stealing hug.

His body is as hard as it looks.

Kenzie grins. "I'm so glad you're here. Mom can hardly wait to see you."

"I look forward to seeing her, too." I felt bad that I had never known what to say to Melissa after Kenzie's dad had left her for another woman. I had seen the complete devastation that had come over her, and aside from bringing over casseroles my mom had ordered the cook to make, I had offered little in the way of comfort to both my best friend and her mom.

At least I could make up for my lack of knowing what to do now.

Kenzie glances past me to Deklan and they share a smile. I wonder what that smile is about, or if she's just happy to see me.

Linking her arm in mine, we start walking and fall into step. It's like the months we were apart are melting away by the second. I've never hung out with a guy like Deklan before, and it's pretty evident from people's expressions that they're interested in him, or more noticeably, the tattoos. Men, women, girls, boys, everyone is staring at him. I wonder if it ever drives Kenzie crazy. If it were me, I think I might get a little jealous or maybe a little insecure about all the attention he gets.

I have to give the boy credit though—he is all about his woman. Ever attentive, he is always the gentleman.

Kenzie and I chat while Deklan effortlessly lifts my sixty-pound designer cheetah-print suitcase from the carousel.

"You weren't kidding, were you?" I murmur, noting the women, both young and old, who are staring at Deklan with open curiosity as he lifts the handle of the suitcase and walks toward us. "Doesn't it drive you bat-shit crazy how people stare at him?"

Kenzie grins. "A little, but I'm growing used to it."

My friend handles herself beautifully though. She smiles as he takes her hand and in turn she takes my hand with the other. We walk out of the airport and across the six lanes of traffic to the parking garage.

Deklan listens to us as we chatter and enter the elevator in the parking garage. When we arrive on the third level, we walk out. Sitting on the concrete barrier is a stunningly handsome young man.

His long legs are in front of him, and his arms are braced at his sides.

Seeing us, he stands, and my heart drops to my toes.

Oh my God.

This is Joshua Ryder.

The infamous, womanizing, asshole Ryder.

No wonder Kenzie was so torn between these two men.

Ryder is nearly as tall as Deklan, has a nice body, but again, he's not as broad shouldered as Deklan…but the boy has a face that would make angels weep.

His gaze travels over me slowly, and when his eyes meet mine I see a gleam in them. An expectation. He's one of those guys who waits for a woman's reaction.

Like he expects me to drop my panties on the spot.

Fat chance, homeboy…

I force my gaze away from him.

"Ryder, this is Ange," Deklan says.

Kenzie's fingers tighten around mine, and she squeezes it.

Apparently she's expecting me to be nice.

I force a smile I don't feel. "Nice to meet you, Ryder," I say, when what I really want to do is kick him in the nuts for the hell he's put my friend through.

This man had hurt my best friend. Granted, Kenzie was now with his best friend, and I'm sure that didn't feel great, but still…the damage he had done in the short time they had been together had been so destructive.

Such a selfish prick.

The phone call I'd received from Kenzie the night she'd caught him sleeping with Sadie had been devastating. I had known how much she had liked Ryder, and how close she had come to giving up her virginity for him.

Thank God she had shown up at his house that night.

"Hey Ange," he says, extending a hand.

I so badly want to tell him that only friends call me Ange, but I bite back the remark. I have no reason to hate this man. He's one of Kenzie's friends and Deklan's best friend, so it's not like he's going anywhere. I had to get used to being in his company.

I take his hand, shake it quickly, and give little more than a quick squeeze before releasing it.

I think he rolls his eyes a split second before he pulls me in for a hug that is entirely too intimate.

Christ, where were his manners, and is that his junk I feel pressed against my stomach?

Ewww…

I think I hear Kenzie laugh behind me, and my cheeks turn pink.

I never blush!

Wedging a hand between us, I manage to push away from him.

His laughter at once is taunting and knowing.

When I turn around, I'm relieved to see that Deklan

has my suitcase in the trunk and is opening the back door for us with a wide smile.

Such a gentleman. Crazy how two best friends can be so different.

Ryder

Ange is not at all what I expected. I had imagined a carbon copy of Kenzie. Girl next door, easy-going, jean-wearing, tank top kind of girl who can mix in with the crowd.

Instead, girlfriend here seems a bit uptight. She practically clings to the grab handle above the door window in her effort not to touch me as we take a sharp left turn. I shift a little and move my leg closer. A heavy sigh follows and then she makes busy going through her purse with her free hand.

Almond-shaped green eyes, tiny nose, and wide, full lips, Ange is attractive, though admittedly not exactly the type I go for. My girls aren't so…frigid.

Deklan would argue that any girl walking is my type, and I can't argue with him.

One of those full lips lifts the slightest bit, and I shake away a nasty vision of what she could do with that mouth. Then again, hadn't I heard her name and virgin used in the same sentence?

I always liked a challenge.

She's of average height, slender, and has an amazing ass that even a sundress can't hide. Her tits are small…maybe a handful, and they fit her body perfectly.

Her brows lift as I pull my gaze back to her face. Her gaze shifts abruptly to my package and lingers for a full ten seconds. I won't lie. I'm surprised by the obvious gesture and am more than a little turned on as I fight back a smile.

"How does that feel?" she says, and when her gaze meets mine, she is not happy.

"Look all you want," I say, arms wide open. "I have nothing to hide."

She rolls her eyes.

I like her spunk.

Too bad she fucking hates me.

But she'll warm to me. Everybody does.

Her firm thighs are so tightly pressed together, I probably couldn't pry them open with a crowbar.

Ange had a serious attitude and screamed high-maintenance.

I'd seen the size of her gargantuan suitcase with the HEAVY tag.

My family was upper middle class, so I didn't want for anything really, but I'd heard the stories of where Kenzie and Ange came from.

They had the kind of money that bought you some level of relief and happiness. And their upper-middle class was in an entirely different hemisphere from Vancouver's upper-middle class. "So, is this your first trip to the Portland area?"

Ange barely turns her head. "Yes, it is."

"I understand you were offered a trip to Hawaii?" I couldn't keep the sarcasm from my voice.

She looks surprised that I knew.

Clearing her throat, she says, "My best friend is here, so yes, I chose to see my best friend, who I haven't seen in seven months, over going to Hawaii for a month with my family."

I frown. "Why would you pass up paradise over Washington? Don't get me wrong, I love where I live…but palm trees and long lazy walks on the beach sound pretty amazing."

"You forget that we have beaches and palm trees in San Diego. You get used to it after a while."

Her tone alone makes me feel like an idiot. "We have a time share there," she says, managing to sound bored. "It's not as great as it sounds, really. Actually, it's a bit too remote for my tastes."

And I bet her tastes were expensive as hell.

"Yeah, I'm sure it really sucks having a second home in Hawaii."

"A time share," she repeats, like she's embarrassed to have more than one home.

"Ange's family has homes in Colorado Springs, New York, Miami, and Paris," Kenzie adds.

I whistle between my teeth, and I'm surprised to see Ange looking embarrassed. I half expected her to be smug.

"They're all time shares...except for Colorado Springs. It used to be my grandparents' house and my dad inherited it just last year."

I pat her hand. "You don't need to explain. I get that your family is filthy rich."

"I'm not trying to explain anything to you," she snaps, ripping her hand from under mine and folding it in her lap.

Whoa. Without meaning to, I had hit a nerve.

She stares out the window the rest of the way home, only turning to look at Kenzie. The two reminisce and I slide down in the seat and watch Ange from the corner of my eye. Every once in a while she'll glance over at me, and I slowly look away.

Deklan plays tour guide as we drive past the old fort and barracks, and Ange seems intrigued, soaking it all in and even taking a picture on her phone.

Her smile slides a little as we pull into the driveway of Deklan's house. She looks...confused.

Kenzie looks back at her. "This is where Deklan and Ryder live."

Is that relief I see in her eyes? "Oh right—with two other band mates."

Ange clears her throat. "What a beautiful older home... and such a quaint neighborhood."

Was this bitch for real?

Deklan is out of the car instantly and opening the back door for Ange.

"We're not heading to your place?" Ange asks when Kenzie follows Deklan inside.

"You don't mind, do you?" Kenzie says. "I'd like you to meet Curtis."

Ange manages a smile. It's obvious she would prefer to leave. "I don't mind at all."

She looked like she might leave her things in the car, then thought better of it. She actually brought the carry-on in. I was surprised she didn't ask to pop the trunk and bring her suitcase as well.

She catches my gaze and frowns.

Once inside, I meet up with Deklan in the kitchen.

"So…what do you think?" he asks, grabbing a few sodas.

"I think she hates me."

Giving me a sympathetic smile, Deklan puts a hand on my shoulder. "Don't worry, man. In time she'll come to love you."

THREE

A^{nge}

The second we pull out of Deklan's driveway, I glance at the older home where Kenzie's boyfriend is waving goodbye to us. Beside him is Ryder. He is obviously too cool to wave, of course. Hands in pockets, he watches with a brooding stare.

I've little doubt he's talking mad shit about me. It's been a taxing few hours having to hang out with the four of us together. I had a pretty good intuition when it came to people, and it was easy to tell that Ryder hated being the third wheel in the Deklan/Kenzie relationship. A few times, I saw his gaze linger a little too long on my best friend. I don't think Deklan realized just how much his friend still liked Kenzie, or if he did, he wasn't acting like it bothered him too much.

Despite the fact that Deklan looked like a dangerous

guy, he was just a really nice guy wrapped in ink. The hair and the piercings just added to his edge.

"You really love him, don't you?"

Kenzie smiles and laughs under her breath. "Oh Ange, you have no idea."

"Oh, I think I do. I've known your every crush since you were eight, and you've never been so head-over-heels."

"What do you think of him?"

I knew my opinion mattered to her. "He's amazing, and oh my God, crazy gorgeous."

"I know, right!"

She beams and squeezes my hand. "He makes me feel…protected. Like when I'm with him I can do anything, or face anything. And it's nice to have a guy in my life that I can depend upon." The grin slowly fades from her lips, and I immediately feel her pain.

"Have you talked to your dad at all?" Kenzie had shared every detail about her parents' divorce with me, and I had ached for her and her mom. I'd been furious with Kenzie's dad, and I had watched the divorce's effect on my own parents. My mom, who was one to nag when she didn't get her way, had nagged a little less and kept a shorter leash on my dad.

She shakes her head. "No. Honestly, I just don't have anything to say to him. He's a selfish prick who thinks only of himself."

"But you must miss him."

"I do, but I missed him more when I first moved here, and it's not as hard as it used to be. That old saying about time healing wounds is true…as cliché as that sounds."

"I bet."

"I just hate that he reached out to Cole and not to me. That was like a kick in the gut. Almost like another betrayal, you know?"

I nod.

Kenzie and her father had always been close. In fact,

she'd been a self-professed daddy's girl. The whole situation was bizarre. "Maybe he just didn't know how you'd respond. You're the one living with your mom, so he probably feels that your loyalty lies with her."

"And my loyalty does lie with her." She released a heavy sigh. "I just don't see the need to talk to him right now."

"I'm sure he misses you just as much as you miss him, Kenz. He's your dad. You need him in your life."

"He's going to be a dad again. He'll have a do-over with his new family. As far as I'm concerned, I don't need him in my life."

I could tell she was over it, and I wouldn't push it... even if I hoped she'd change her mind in the future.

"I respect that."

"You don't know what it's like." I barely heard the statement, but it was there. "I mean all of it. After he left us, it's like everything I knew no longer existed. I had to start over completely and learn a new normal."

"And you did it...with grace. I tell you, even Sister Frieda would be proud."

The corners of her mouth twitched.

Sister Frieda had been our etiquette coach. Her catchphrase had been, 'Go forth with grace and dignity.'

I drop any mention of Kenzie's father and make a mental note to put the topic on the back burner, or until such a time she wanted to talk about it. She takes a left onto a city block, past businesses, and then takes a few more turns before pulling over in front of a bunch of older brick homes that appeared to have been converted into apartments.

"We have arrived at our final destination," she says, pushing the car door open.

I follow her line of vision to one of the identical apartments on the block.

"Don't look so stunned, Ange. I warned you to lower your expectations before you came here."

I do everything I can to school my features. When

Kenzie told me she and her mom had moved into a downtown apartment in Vancouver, a cute little bedroom community of Portland, I had thought more high-rise looking out over the Portland lights apartment and less...well, no view, and a city bus stop outside the front door. How was this even possible after the lifestyle they'd had in San Diego?

I could only hope the inside was an improvement.

It wasn't.

Setting my suitcase in the hallway/landing/dining room of the apartment, I couldn't help recalling the mansion on the beach that Kenzie had, until recently, called home for the majority of her life. They'd even had servants.

I'm not going to lie—I was shocked.

There was a living room off to the left, with an old brick fireplace with no gas insert. The light fixtures were all standard old-school brass. The place hadn't had a facelift since before I was born.

As usual, Kenzie's mom Melissa had decorated the tiny, depressing space to perfection, giving it her own stamp. The tiny kitchen had a host of issues, most of all ancient appliances, but again she'd worked her magic and did a great job at making it homey. Those small touches were familiar and put me slightly more at ease.

I eye the door. There was just a standard lock and a deadbolt.

"You're judging me, aren't you?" Kenzie asks, grabbing a plastic container out of the fridge and prying the lid off. She smells whatever it is, puts the lid back on, and places it back in the fridge untouched. I can't tell if she's upset by my reaction. She picks a grape off a cluster and pops it into her mouth.

"No, of course not." I take a deep breath and wish now that I'd kept my mouth shut about her clearly irresponsible father. I mean, what a complete asshole. I am sooooo tempted to snap a picture and send it to my mother. She'd change her tune about wanting Kenzie to reconcile with her father immediately upon seeing how my best friend and her mom were living. My mom wouldn't last five seconds in the apartment. In fact, she'd once spent a week at a luxury resort when one of her eight bathrooms was being renovated because she 'didn't want to deal with the noise'.

Speaking of noise—was that a window air-conditioner making that sound?

Oh my God…it was. I was astounded just how far they had fallen in such a short amount of time.

It was all I could do not to get on the phone and call my mom to tell her to wire funds immediately. How dare that douchebag of a dad leave them living in such conditions? It was completely unfair, especially given the fact he'd just returned from a private island getaway with his new trophy wife.

No wonder Kenzie was so pissed at her dad. He'd left his wife and youngest child living in what I could only guess was the armpit of Vancouver. As if to validate my point, an old lady in a dirty trench coat with a raggedy-looking dog walked past the apartment just as a city bus pulled up.

I am beyond appalled.

I straighten my shoulders, determined to help the two of them out of this mess they found themselves in. "Where is your mom?"

"At work. She should be home anytime. Do you want to see the rest of the apartment?"

It takes less than thirty seconds to see the bathroom and two bedrooms.

I stood in the doorway of Kenzie's room, relieved to see she had the friendship collage we'd made our freshman year hanging on the wall, along with pictures of her Vancouver friends. "If there are just two rooms, then where does Cole sleep when he visits?"

"When he's here, he crashes on the hide-a-bed."

"When he's here? I thought he was home for the summer." I hope my disappointment isn't completely obvious. I've been in love with Cole for years. Ever since he walked into Kenzie's room with low riding jeans on and no shirt. I was only thirteen at the time, but holy crap did I want him after that. Every single time he walked into a room, my heart would start to hammer like it would pound right out of my chest. I'd never told Kenzie about my obsession with her brother. I guess I'd just assumed one day she would catch on.

She never had. Or if she had, she had never said a word.

So I'd suffered on in silence, saying nothing to anyone.

"He'll be here in a few days. Lucky for me, he spends a lot of time running back and forth to Seattle."

My heart rate speeds up. He'll be home in a few days. Yes! "How come he's running back and forth?"

"Football stuff, I guess," she says, sounding bored.

I look at the collage and smile. "We were such dorks, weren't we?" I missed those days. Little did we realize how much life would change in a matter of years, with a happy family shattered and one of us plucked from the other's life so abruptly.

Kenzie put her arm around my shoulder. "So, are you ready for me to take you back to the airport so you can escape this nightmare?"

"Don't be ridiculous," I say with a smile, looking around the room that would be my home for the next five weeks. "We're going to have the summer of our lives."

FOUR

Ryder

"For the record, this is not a double-date," Ange says the second I opened the car door for her.

We are at the movies—a chick-flick that I have been dragged along to. Deklan said he wanted me along because he wants me to keep Ange company, but I know it's more because he doesn't trust me when it comes to using drugs.

It had been ten days since I'd last used and I thought I would be feeling better by now. I would wake up feeling on top of the world, and within an hour or two I was ready to rip someone's throat out. Sensing my agitation, Deklan had suggested we go for a run this morning and we had. I'll admit the run had helped until we got back home.

When we stopped by *Branded* to put the supply shipment away, Bags, an old friend of mine nicknamed for the bags of drugs he sold, had walked in. He'd lingered, looking at one of about twenty photo albums stuffed full of tattoo designs sitting on the bookshelves.

He must have gotten the idea that I wasn't interested, because he'd eventually left.

Deklan kept an eye on him the entire time, so now every single time I turn around, there's Dek—up my ass, looking over my shoulder and asking me what I'm doing.

I swear life at my parents' house would be less invasive.

"Where do you want to sit?" Deklan asks Kenzie.

There were only four other people in the theater.

"Let's go a few rows down at least." Kenzie and Deklan sit down. Ange plops beside Kenzie, and I sit beside her.

She sighs heavily and for a second I can tell she is considering moving to Deklan's other side. Instead, she leans back and settles in, but only for a second. For the next few minutes she adjusts everything around her—taking a water bottle from her purse, setting it in the holder, meticulously unfolding four napkins and placing them over her lap so that not one square inch of her white capri jeans will be soiled by the buttery popcorn on her lap.

Three middle-school age girls take their seats directly in front of us.

"Seriously?" Ange says underneath her breath, her irritation obvious.

A cute Oriental girl with braces glances back at me, her gaze sweeping from me to Deklan, then back to me. I give her a wink and she turns to her friends and they break into giggles.

Ange shakes her head in disgust.

"I vote for moving right now, because I don't want to deal with giggling throughout the entire movie." Ange makes no effort to lower her voice and the girls hear her. They send her nasty glances over their shoulders.

I smile at them and three sets of eyes widen as they grin back at me.

It's like taking candy from a baby, and I like how the

attention, even if it is from young girls, just pisses Ange off even more.

Ange leans against me, her lips next to my ear. "They're children, you know."

"I'm well aware of that. I have a brother who is twelve." Just talking about my brother makes my heart squeeze. I hate that I can't see him. My mom won't allow it. If I ever 'get my shit together', then I can have the pleasure of my family's company, but until then…I'm destined to live life without them.

That information that I have a little brother seems to surprise her.

"You were once that age, you know."

"Yes, and not that long ago. I know guys like you, Ryder. You're dangerous to little girls."

Like I would go for a thirteen year-old, and I almost say the words out loud but I stop. Instead, I turn my head the slightest bit, and she's forced to ease away, but we're still very close. "Are you a little girl, Ange? Am I *dangerous* to you?"

I look for any ounce of arousal or interest in those green eyes but there's none. Just the same irritation I've seen since I met her.

Have I lost my touch?

"Dude, you are so barking up the wrong tree."

I frown, seriously wondering what I did to her. "Batting for the other team, are you? Hmm, I wouldn't have ever guessed that, but I do like a challenge."

The sides of her mouth lift, but the false smile doesn't begin to touch her eyes. "For the record, no, I'm not batting for the other team, not that there's anything wrong with that. Love is love."

Oh shit. Here we go. "Calm down. I agree with you. I have a cousin who is gay and he's the nicest guy on the planet. His boyfriend is a dick, but what do you do? He's in love."

She bites her lip, and I know she's refraining from

throwing my own words back at me. Does she really think I'm such a prick?

As the minutes tick by and I remain silent, she seems to settle down a bit. My gaze shifts to that mouth and those lips that are straight-up amazing.

She mouths the word *asshole* and I can't help myself—I laugh.

Her brows furrow as I reach over and take a handful of her popcorn.

A piece falls from the bag onto the napkin, conveniently on the V of her inner thighs. I reach for it, but she blocks me. "Don't…even…think…about…it."

"Can't blame a guy for trying."

"Ewwww." She takes the popcorn, tosses it on the floor, then proceeds to pull out a bottle of sanitizer from her purse and squirt some in her hand.

I slouch down in my seat. This chick is unbelievable.

The movie starts and I spread my legs wide.

Ange immediately stiffens and straightens, shoulders like a board.

"Have you heard of personal space?"

"As in your personal," I say, looking specifically at her boobs then shifting my gaze lower. "Space."

She lifts her chin. "Wow, you are just really something else."

"That's what they say. You want to give me a try?"

Closing her eyes, she takes a deep breath and releases it slowly.

"Practicing yoga?"

"Actually, I'm practicing patience, and I need a butt-load of it with you."

"I love it when you talk dirty."

The movie starts and she lifts a hand. "I'd like to enjoy the movie rather than debate with you."

I lean toward her. "You smell amazing, by the way."

A nge

Seriously. I've never met anyone who is so irritating. I can't even enjoy the movie because Ryder keeps watching me from the corner of his eye. I try to act nonchalant, to relax and enjoy the film, but with Ryder's own personal fan club sitting in front of us, it's impossible to get into the movie. It's all I can do to not move to another seat, far away from him, and yet if I move, then he wins…and I will never let Ryder win.

Thank God the movie is halfway decent, although the parts where the main couple are having sex has me shifting in my seat and feeling all kinds of uncomfortable.

Strangely, I remember when Kenzie told me about the first night she and Ryder had made out after watching her dirty dance with Sadie, the slut who had slept with Ryder when Kenzie had been dating him.

Kenzie had done a complete play-by-play about what happened in Deklan's bedroom. The image had been imprinted in my mind, and we had giggled like the middle-school girls who are currently sitting in front of us.

For a split second, I imagine making out with Ryder.

What the hell is wrong with me?

It was just the movie making me wish I had a boyfriend.

The scene was smoking hot and had the girls in front of us laughing and sneaking glances over their shoulder at Ryder and Deklan.

I catch Kenzie's gaze and she grins.

I'm glad it doesn't bother her.

Kenzie and Deklan hold hands through the entire movie, and every once in a while he would lean over and kiss her. I feel a strange stab of envy. During the few days I'd been in Vancouver, I'd reconnected with Kenz and I loved it—loved having my best friend back, and yet it was bizarre to have Deklan around. And when he worked or had practice, she constantly checked her phone and smiled every time she received a message or a call.

He was the center of her universe and it was tough to compete with that.

I had yet to meet Brooke. Tonight the family would get together when Cole arrived.

My stomach had been tied in knots all day. I was both excited and nervous to meet the band that had become such a part of my best friend's life.

When the movie finally ends, I'm relieved. I just want to get back to the apartment, put on my sweats, and get away from Mr. Overconfident.

"So Kenzie's brother is coming home tonight, huh?"

My stomach tightens. "Yes."

***

Five hours later, I'm standing in the living room of Kenzie's apartment.

My heart is pounding so loud I'm sure everyone in the room can hear it.

Cole will be arriving any second.

Ryder sits sprawled in a chair, inhaling the tortilla chips and salsa like it's his last meal. Of all people to be present tonight...

I'm so sick of his face, and of all nights for him to be here—it has to be the night I'm reunited with Cole.

I feel someone staring at me from across the room.

Kenzie's cousin Brooke. She's territorial about her friendship with Kenzie, letting me know at every opportunity that they're family, so therefore they have a special bond. Not that she said it, but she didn't need to. Her fuck you attitude speaks volumes. You'd think with them being family and all she'd be less that way, but I can tell by the short conversation we had that she wasn't thrilled that I had shown up.

Every time I start a sentence with "remember the time...," Brooke follows it up with her own story about something she and Kenzie had done, and it would always trump whatever Kenzie and I had done.

So annoying.

My attention is diverted when Kenzie leans back against Deklan and his arms slide around her. He places a kiss on the top of her head and she smiles up at him. Her mom gives me a wink and I'm surprised that the woman I had known in San Diego has become so open and accepting of her daughter and her tattooed, pierced boyfriend. Months ago, Melissa would have locked Kenzie in her room and forbade her to see someone who looked like Deklan. Granted, the boyfriend treats her like a princess. Still, I know how rough it must be to let go of the little girl who she used to keep on such a tight leash.

Proof that they had both changed a lot since the time they had left San Diego.

Melissa's phone rings and she tells everyone to be quiet. "Hello." She nods. "Okay, we'll see you shortly." She hangs up the phone, her excitement obvious. "That was Shelly. They're just blocks away." She crosses the room and checks the blinds.

There are only nine of us here, but already the room feels crowded.

I slide trembling hands over my skirt, wondering if I should have maybe worn jeans instead. The length isn't too short, so it's not like I'm showing too much thigh. I did get a brow arch from Ryder when I walked out of Kenzie's room though. Then again, any girl with a pulse no doubt excites him.

I kicked my wedges off at the last minute and gone with flat sandals. I didn't want to look like I was working too hard at it.

Now I kind of wish I had the wedges back on. A girl always looked better in heels, my mom had told me the first time I shopped in Rodeo Drive with her. I had been in kindergarten.

I stop myself from going back and putting the wedges on. No one else would notice, but Ryder definitely would. He'll give me that smirky smile that makes me think he can read my every thought.

Ryder removes his hand from the now-empty chip bowl, wipes his fingers on his leg, and stands slowly. He's watching me as I watch the front door expectantly.

Damn him. He is such a thorn in my side.

I slide a hand through my perfectly curled hair and I swear I hear him snicker. I glance at him and sure enough, he's looking right at me…or rather at what bit of leg I am showing.

Asshole.

I hear Cole's footsteps as he comes up the steps. His voice is music to my ears. He's laughing at something his aunt is saying, and then the door opens.

"Surprise!" everyone yells, except for me. The word sticks in my throat and it comes out as a strange, strangled sound instead.

Cole drops his duffel bag on the floor and is beaming at his mom, who runs into his arms.

I've seen pictures of him online but I'm not prepared for what seeing him in person does to me, or how it makes me feel.

His blonde hair is a bit more so, and he has a nice tan. His body is as chiseled as I remember.

When he sets his mom back on her feet, he greets each person warmly. My heart is pounding out of my chest as he greets his sister and Deklan. He's clearly already seen pictures of Deklan because there is no surprise on his face. They shake hands and he gives Kenz a nice hug. He turns to me. "Ange, look at you. I like the hair."

"Hey," I manage to choke out, and then his arms are sliding around me and I'm in his embrace.

It's heaven, being smothered against his broad chest. The hug was unexpected and I'm horrified when I see that my lip gloss is on the collar of his shirt.

"Sorry," I say while trying to wipe the stain off with my thumb.

"No worries," he replies with a grin that makes me feel like my insides are made of warm butter.

Suddenly all my thoughts and cares fade away and all is right with the world again.

FIVE

R^{yder}

The change that overcomes Ange the second Cole walks into the apartment is pretty amazing to watch. Little Miss Serious is grinning from ear to ear and I'm surprised to see deep dimples on either side of that amazing mouth of hers. She's beaming nearly as much as Kenzie's mom is.

She looks like a kid on Christmas morning.

The only one who doesn't look overly enthusiastic to see Cole is Kenzie. Her smile is forced, and I know the feeling of inadequacy that comes over her expression as she watches her mother and sibling hug for the fifth time. Melissa is practically gushing all over her star athlete son.

Deklan takes a seat on the sofa nearest to me.

Kenzie and Ange are talking and no doubt it's about golden boy, who with his puffed out chest is savoring his homecoming.

His aunt gives him a forceful hug, Brooke manages a pat on the shoulder, and Kenzie gives her brother a quick embrace. Mr. Star Athlete gives us the once-over before he walks our way.

"Nice of you to come."

"I wouldn't miss it," Deklan says, and I have to stop myself from calling bullshit. Granted, I do think my best friend wants to support his girl in everything, but family gatherings have always been just a little too cozy for Deklan. It's hard enough to deal with my own family drama, let along someone else's, but my buddy is motivated to impress his girl's family, and so I will do everything I possibly can to help him.

"You're Ryder?" Cole sticks out a hand. It's obvious the guy is a gym rat by the size of his biceps.

"That's right."

His grip just about brings me to my knees. It's intentional and I squeeze right back, hoping to make him wince, but instead he's amused, his lips quirking in overconfidence.

"You still in high school?"

I straighten up and lift my chin a good inch. "No, I graduated."

"Which college are you attending?"

"I'm not sure," I say, and his brow arches.

He stares at me and I know he's judging me. I've become used to that expression from everyone around me lately.

"What's the plan if the rockstar gig doesn't work out?"

Beside me, Deklan shifts on his feet. He's ready to defend me—just like he has always done.

"Probably the same as yours if your NFL plans don't work out." The words are out before I can recant them.

I glance at Deklan, and there's the slightest quirk on his lips that he covers as he lifts a bottle of water to his mouth.

Goddamn jocks. They think they rule the world. Ironically, some of them are the biggest drug abusers I know.

Cole smirks and after a few stabs at conversation, he

moves over to Ange. His voice is jovial, even a little flirty.

And she's practically gushing. Jesus, why doesn't she just lie on her back and get it over with already?

"Forty-five minutes max and we're out of here," Brooke says, dropping beside me on the loveseat.

There's the girl I know and love. You never had to question what Brooke was thinking. She always spoke her mind.

"Forty-five, really?" I say. "I was hoping for twenty."

"Not long enough," Brooke says, eyeing Ange again. "My mom already told me an hour, and I'm counting the time before golden boy arrived as time served."

We all watch the interaction between Ange and Cole. Am I the only one who sees how Ange is reacting to him?

"So…what do we think of the new arrival?" Brooke asks, sounding as bored as I felt.

"You mean Cole?" I ask.

She frowns. "No…I meant Ange."

Deklan takes a drink of punch. "I think she's nice."

"Must you always be so diplomatic?" It's obvious Brooke isn't as big a fan of Ange as Deklan is.

"She's alright," I add, and the answer seems to please her because she grins. "A bit straight-laced, and it's so obvious that she's got the hots for Cole."

Brooke's brows lift.

How could I be the only one to realize how much Ange wants her cousin?

"Oh my God, you're right. Look at her. She's blushing."

And Ange's eyes were bright with excitement. Of course she would be beaming, with jock boy giving her his full attention.

Brooke snorts. "No doubt by week's end he will be creeping into her bedroom. You want to place bets?"

Normally I'd be amused and interested in placing such a wager, and yet the idea, and image, of Ange being plowed by Mr. Pro Athlete completely irritates the shit out of me.

What the hell?

I have to get laid. It's the only explanation why I'm suddenly so pissed off. I was tired of jerking off in the shower, and if I was getting all worked up about a stuck-up socialite getting banged by a gym rat, then I had issues.

A nge

I'm so relieved when the guests leave and it's just me, Kenzie, Melissa, and Cole. Granted, I liked Brooke well enough, and she seemed to be nicer the second Curtis had shown up. I'm always amazed with a strong-willed girl is with a guy who is so laid back and easy going.

Even Ryder played nice, though every single time I looked his way, he was staring at me, watching me, especially when Cole came up to talk to me. I felt those blue eyes on me the entire time.

Now Ryder's gone, thank God, and I can relax.

I'm in my pajamas in the living room, watching the end of a sitcom with Cole, Kenzie, and Melissa. I couldn't give a summary of what I'd just watched if my life depended on it. I'm too busy paying attention to Cole.

Wearing a pair of cargo shorts, he's sitting on the couch, his arm along the back of it. Melissa is beside him, and Kenzie beside her, knees up to her chest, leaning toward the end table. Her body language spoke volumes.

Despite the obvious unhappiness in my friend's life, I'm elated to be here, in this moment, with my best friend and her gorgeous brother. It's been nearly a year since we've seen each other and I'm happy he's been so welcoming.

Melissa covers a yawn with her hand and announces she's calling it a night. "Do you need help with the hide-a-bed?" she asks, motioning to the sheets, blankets, and pillows piled on the chair nearest the television.

"Nah, Mom, I have it. Thanks for the nice homecoming,"

he says. "I loved the apple pie."

"You're welcome, sweetie," she says, kissing him on the top of the head before walking past me and Kenzie, stopping almost as an afterthought to give her daughter a squeeze on the shoulder with her hand.

I feel Kenzie's disappointment that she didn't receive the same sign of affection from her mom, and I know that Melissa doesn't realize that the small things, like kissing her son and not her daughter, have helped make Kenzie feel the way she does about her brother.

The resentment has been building for a lifetime and one day I'm afraid it will be too much to work through.

Yet another reason I'm sad her dad isn't in her life. They had been close, and now that he's buddied up with Cole, it makes the betrayal that much more intense. Kenzie hasn't said as much, but she doesn't need to.

"We should go to bed," Kenzie says, stretching. It has been a long day, and yet I don't want it to end just yet. It seems like I've been waiting forever to see him.

"Help me make this thing up," Cole says, already standing and tossing the pillows off the couch onto the loveseat.

Kenzie helps him pull out the hide-a-bed, and I set about making the bed. I can feel Cole's gaze on me. I might have bent over a little more than I should, showing him more thigh than I would normally.

When I glance up, he's staring at my ass.

A warm tingling rushes through me. I'm ecstatic. I like that he's looking at me, watching me with a glint in his eyes that I have never seen before.

That look both excites and scares me.

If he asks me to stay and watch television with him, I might be half tempted to hang out with him, just as long as it doesn't upset Kenzie.

I finish tucking the sheets in and fluff a pillow for good measure. "Good night, Cole."

"Night ladies," he says, and when I glance back over my shoulder, my heart gives a lurch when I realize he's staring at me. He gives me a wink and I grin, elated by his response.

SIX

R^{yder}

The strobe lights are giving me a headache…and for some reason I can't play for shit.

The guitar feels odd in my hands, and my mind is everywhere but on the song.

I'm so fucking distracted.

Brooke keeps looking over at me, but I focus my gaze on the crowd, mainly the brunette in the front row with the huge tits that are coming out of her barely-there tank dress every time she jumps in time to the music.

Her gaze never wavers from mine through the entire song. Not once. I swear she barely blinks.

The venue is new to our band *The Frozen*, and I'm not sure I really like that the majority of the audience is sitting on their butts and aren't piling in around us like our normal crowd.

There's something comforting in having appreciative fans clamoring to get to the front and center of the stage. Aside from the chicks in the audience standing, clapping, and jumping, the rest of the crowd appears to be waiting for the main act.

I'm struggling. I know that, and I want to use more than ever. Or get so fucking drunk I can't see straight. I hate, and almost resent, the fact that every single one of my friends has found a new lease on life in their sobriety and yet I'm still waiting for the sky to open so I can have a fucking epiphany about what I'm supposed to do with the rest of my life.

Deklan has it made. At twenty-two, he's already managed to get a loyal following as one of the Portland/ Vancouver's most popular tattoo artists. He has a month long waiting list for clients, and I admit, I'm envious that he's found what he's passionate about. He's set for life and already has a rock star tattoo artist status in the community. Some people never find one thing they're passionate about, and yet he'd already managed to find two.

At the encouragement of his big brother, Curtis has decided to take business courses at the community college.

My dad would give anything for me to say I'd go to college and follow in his footsteps as an accountant, just like his father and his father before him.

Fuck that shit. I'd rather die than work with figures day in and day out.

Honestly, me in a suit and tie, sitting in an office of some business district just wouldn't fly. I wouldn't be able to breathe.

I may not know what I did want, but I definitely know what I didn't want. I didn't want to be an unemployed, no talent loser with a drug problem that followed me into my adult life.

I hit yet another wrong note and cringe.

Brooke walks toward me, and as I focus on playing the

riff, she rests her hand on my shoulder. Her fingers squeeze tight, and I read a lot into that gesture. *Get your shit together now.*

I glance at her and she leans in until our lips are inches away. Except it's not out of adoration that she's making it look like we're about to make out. No, her eyes are full of rage as her gaze burns into mine.

The crowd erupts in applause as she grabs my face and proceeds to lick me from chin to ear. I have to hand it to her—the chick is a master, and I admire her for her drive and determination. She has true talent. Maybe that's part of my problem. The band has already proven they can play without me. They've done it before and replaced me with Terry, Curtis's brother, more times than I could count when I'd bailed on them.

"You're all over the place," Brooke whispers in my ear before belting out the chorus. She walks back toward the other side of the stage to plant a kiss on her boyfriend. Curtis, who probably wanted to kill me two seconds ago when his woman was licking my face, now eats up the attention his woman is bestowing on him.

My gaze is suddenly averted. Just beyond Curtis, waiting in the wings, are Kenzie and Ange. They aren't like the majority of the chicks in the crowd who wear sleazy outfits to get our attention.

Both are dressed in jeans and sexy tank tops. Earlier I'd noticed that Ange's tank shows off the majority of her athletic back. She's sexy in an effortless way.

"Ryder!" I hear my name being screamed from the direction of the brunette. She is dancing in her seat, and I swear she lifts up the edge of her skirt a good few inches. Taut thighs, nice high ass. It has been weeks since I've had sex. With the watchdog known as Deklan tracking my every move, it doesn't help my near celibate status. Also, I haven't really been too interested.

Now I'm definitely interested, especially since it's being

dangled before me like a carrot on a string.

I jump when Brooke's voice comes from right behind me. Jesus Christ, she is all over me tonight, and she isn't happy. I can't blame her. In fact, I'm sure she's not the only one who is going to grill me the second I step off the stage.

"Thank you, Portland!" she yells into the microphone. I'm secretly glad there isn't time for an encore.

Not that this crowd wanted one from us.

I unplug my bass and give a pointed look at the brunette as I make my way off the stage. Kenzie runs past me into Deklan's arms and I glance at Ange. She doesn't make eye contact with me.

I don't wait for my bandmates and make a right into the hallway.

The brunette is there and she's alone.

I take her by the hand and we walk briskly down the dark, dingy hallway. I don't know the venue that well. "Where can we go?" I ask, my voice coming out gruffer than I wanted.

Her dark eyes widen…and I kiss her softly on the lips. She smiles and whispers, "Follow me."

She doesn't have to say it twice.

We take a right down another dingy hallway and straight into a small room full of cleaning supplies. There is a single light bulb hanging from the ceiling with a shoestring tied to it. I yank on the string and the dim light barely gives off any illumination.

"Do you have any drugs?" The words are out before I can stop them.

Her brows lift and she reaches into her purse and rifles through her wallet. My heart actually misses a beat as I wait for what she's going to reveal. She produces a yellow oval pill, bites down and swallows half before slipping the other half between her teeth.

I lean in and kiss her, my mouth covering hers, my tongue sliding past her teeth, sweeping the bitter pill into my mouth and swallowing before I kiss her again.

I pull her skirt up, her panties down, and slide my fingers over her dripping sex.

"I can't believe I'm here alone with you," she says, and I bet she's said that to a lot of musicians. How else would she know about this little shithole of a place to disappear into?

I slip a finger inside and she moans.

Her warmth swallows my finger and I slide another in.

She slips her tits out of her dress. Both nipples are pierced, with a silver rod through each.

I dip my head and kiss the tops of her breasts before taking a nipple into my mouth.

"Oh yeah, that feels good," she says, her fingers fisting my hair.

I'm about to explode.

She touches my cock and I suck in a breath.

"Just a sec." She leans down, reaches for something in her purse and produces a condom. Ripping the package open with her teeth, she spits the top out onto the floor, slides the rubber on my cock, then proceeds to push it down with her mouth.

My heart rate picks up speed. Her mouth feels so good on my cock.

I keep my hands on her shoulders and she gets the idea of what I want.

Outside in the hallway I hear people walking by. A few times the door handle is rattled, and it gives me pause... until my friend wiggles.

I can't hold it in for long. It's been a long time since I've had sex, and I close my eyes. I'm almost appalled when Ange's face flashes before me. I imagine her mouth around my cock, those lips sucking me.

I reach down and slide her nipples between my forefinger and thumb, tugging on the little bars. I gently squeeze the erect buds and she lets out a gasp. Her pace picks up and she's motivated to please. It's then I realize that she has one hand on her own sex, where two fingers are buried knuckle deep.

Her free hand grips my ass and she pulls me closer.

I come with a groan and am relieved when she releases a little whimper as she too achieves climax by her own hand.

There's a flash of both triumph and disappointment in her eyes.

She was clearly looking for a lay. I unroll the condom and toss it into the trash. She eyes it, and I have visions of her selling it on eBay. I make a note to lock the door behind us, because I'm not about to stick the used rubber in my pocket.

"There's more where that came from," she says with a satisfied moan. "Maybe I can come over tonight?"

I give her a kiss. "Maybe." I'm tempted, but having any chick over to my makeshift bedroom in Deklan's dungeon is hardly appealing.

I say nothing as we walk out the door a minute later. Down the hall, my band is looking for me. It's Deklan I first make eye contact with. He lifts his head and looks relieved to see me.

Jesus, I couldn't have been gone for five minutes.

The rest of the band follows his gaze and turns to look my way.

At that exact moment, the brunette by my side threads her fingers through mine.

Shit...

Neither Kenzie nor Brooke looks at all surprised that I'm cozy with the brunette. The latter has a smug smile on her lips that quickly turns to a sneer.

I can't say the same for Ange. She frowns at me, and then looks at the brunette at my side. She even mouths the word, "Really?" I'm still mortified I'd thought of her during sex. What the hell. Why would I think of the ice queen?

I walk toward my friends and the entire time Ange's gaze is shifting between my new friend and me.

"Hey," Brooke says. "We've been looking for you."

I glance at the brunette, whose gaze never wavers from Brooke.

"Sorry, I went outside and got some air."

"Isn't that the door to the janitor's closet?" Curtis says innocently enough.

Everyone laughs…except for Ange, who looks at me in disgust.

I glance back and shrug. "I have no idea."

"We ready to head out?" Deklan says, and he's staring into my eyes like he's piercing my fucking soul. There's no way he'll know I took a half of a pill.

I give him a pat on the back and he seems to relax. "Yeah. You alright, buddy?" I ask before he can drill me.

"Yeah. I'm ready when you are."

The brunette pouts. "You're leaving already?"

"Give me your phone number," I say, taking out my phone.

She gives me her number twice. I repeat it back to her for good measure.

"My name's Amber, by the way."

"Seriously?" Ange says. She shakes her head and runs a hand down her face. "Wow."

The band leaves Amber and me alone for a second.

"You have any more of what you gave me?" I ask, brushing back her raven-colored hair with one hand. My thumb lingers on her cheek.

She leans into me and sighs. "Yes."

I give her a soft kiss before she reaches into her purse. She slides the pills into my pocket, her hand coming close to my cock. She flashes a coy smile as she fondles me for a quick second. "Call me, okay?"

"I definitely will."

She clings to me, and for a second I'm tempted to stay… until I think of how shitty I played tonight and how good my bed sounds right about now.

"You sure I can't come by tonight?" She bites her bottom lip and tries her best to look innocent. She's not. I've known her kind before. She'll be back in the third row jumping up and down and flashing her assets to the bassist in the next band.

"I'm exhausted or I would."

When I look up, her friends are waiting for her, their eyes wide with surprise. She flashes them a triumphant smile.

Seeing them, she gives me one more kiss and whispers in my ear. "You're amazing. I can't wait to feel you inside me."

I swallow hard and try not to let the words swell my ego.

As I walk away from her, I hear her friends ask her about me. They gasp and giggle as I turn left. My friends are waiting by the door. They're laughing at something Curtis says, and I smile to myself.

I find the nearest bathroom and once I'm in a stall I check my pocket. I'm almost disappointed to see the familiar oval pills. Hydrocodone.

I need to take all four to get an effect out of them at all.

For a split second, I feel a sense of disappointment in myself. Disappointment that I had played so shitty, and disappointed that I had fucked up twelve days of sobriety.

SEVEN

A nge

Ryder makes me sick to my stomach. He's disgusting.

I so badly want to tell him what I think of him.

The smug look on his face as he walked out of that janitor's closet with his slut on his arm is too much. I'd watched him during the concert and could see the girl give him the eye all night. I was disgraced by my own sex knowing that she'd given it up so easily, and she'd never even told him her name beforehand. I mean, what kind of girl does that?

Curtis asks Ryder the brunette's name and when he gives a lopsided smile, I look away and out at the passing landscape.

Thank God I'm not stuck in the backseat with him.

Ryder becomes all chatty as we drive back into Vancouver, and even the sound of his voice is getting on my nerves.

Deklan is smiling at Ryder like everything that comes out of his mouth is sunshine. I didn't get the connection or why they were even friends. Aside from the band and their mutual love of music, it didn't seem like they had all that much in common. Deklan actually had a talent and a real job. He supported himself and Kenzie had told me he'd already saved up over thirty thousand dollars toward buying his own house one day.

Impressive.

Ryder was just dead weight.

I want to be as far away from him as I can get, and I'm honestly relieved when Kenzie told Deklan that we can only stay for an hour before we have to go home.

An hour is about all I can stomach anyway. Plus, I'm anxious to see what Cole is up to.

Curtis and Brooke are already at the house when we arrive, and Brooke is wearing pajama pants and a hoodie, with her face bare of the makeup she used earlier.

She doesn't look anything like the girl I saw perform on stage in front of two hundred people.

"Hey Ryder, can I talk to you for a second?" she says, motioning for him to follow her into the kitchen where Curtis was standing, holding a mug between his hands.

"If you want to tell me I played like shit, I openly admit it to everyone."

This silences her immediately and she nods. "You did play like shit, and I don't understand, because at practice last night you lit it up."

"Sorry, I just had an off night."

I force a smile I didn't feel. "It happens."

"The brunette with the huge tits didn't help," Curtis says, walking out of the kitchen. Brooke shoots him a look that promised death.

"Sorry babe, but it's the truth," Curtis says with a shrug.

"Oh *really*?" Brooke says, planting her hands on her tiny hips.

Curtis gathers her up in a hug and she gives him a shove. "No, you want a chick with big tits and no brains."

"We don't know that Amber doesn't have any brains." This comes from Ryder, who is quick to defend his groupie.

"Tell me you used a condom?" Curtis remarks.

Ryder's lips quirk.

I'm uncomfortable with the discussion and excuse myself to go to the bathroom.

When I come out, Brooke and Curtis are on the couch watching TV, and Kenzie is waiting for me by the doorway that leads down the stairs to Deklan and Ryder's part of the house.

I'm reminded of a dungeon every time I walk into the place. The only light that ever comes in is by way of a half a dozen windows that I'd be lucky to fit through. I wonder what would happen if there was a fire.

The thought gives me the creeps.

Deklan turns on the television and joins us on the couch. He slides his arm around Kenzie and she snuggles up against him. He immediately starts playing with her hair.

Ryder goes to the bathroom and actually leaves the door open as he pees.

Wow. Seriously, what is this guy's problem?

Kenzie and Deklan are completely unaffected by his lack of modesty.

When he emerges, he sprawls into a recliner.

For some reason my mind is flashing images of what he and that brunette had done in the janitor's closet. Granted, I have never had sex before, but I've heard people talk about it. Plus, I've seen enough movies to imagine how it feels.

I shift and focus my attention on the TV.

He's two feet from me. I glance at him beneath lowered lashes.

Tonight I watched the women in the audience watch him. He knew what he did to the fairer sex, and he oozed with confidence. If he'd played like shit, like Brooke had repeatedly said from the second she'd stepped off stage, I hadn't heard it…but then again, I'm not a musician. I thought they had all done an amazing job. When Kenzie originally told me about *The Frozen*, I imagined a mediocre garage band.

I'd been wrong.

Ryder's place in the band was probably cemented because of his looks and his ability to literally charm the panties off the women in the audience.

He keeps nodding off—no doubt exhausted from his liaison in the closet.

As his eyelids lower, I notice that his eyelashes are obnoxiously long. The boy is entirely too gorgeous for his own good.

I must have sighed because he turns and glances right at me. For ten seconds, he says nothing. He just stares at me.

My heartbeat is pounding in my ears.

The corners of his mouth lift the slightest bit. "You want to sit on my lap, Ange?"

Did he honestly just say that?

I have to seriously be careful around him. He constantly baits me and was always looking for a way to get under my skin.

I scratch my chin with my middle finger and turn my attention back to the TV.

He laughs under his breath and continues to watch me.

My cheeks burn. He's still staring at me, and I can't pretend to act like I don't know he's staring and doing what he can to make me squirm.

And yes, he loves to make me squirm. He's made that obvious from the first day we met.

I resist the urge to tell him to kiss my ass, because I'm sure he'd say gladly…even after doing that girl in the closet at the concert.

I turn to Kenzie, ready to tell her I wanted to go home, but now her head is on Deklan's lap and he's playing with her hair.

Oh my God. Shoot me…

"I'll braid your hair for you." Ryder's brow is lifted high and I see a challenge in those blue eyes.

My gaze shifts to him. His lips are quirked now. He is mocking me. Could he tell in a glance that I envied my friend for having an incredible boyfriend who wasn't at all embarrassed to be playing with her hair? A man who made her feel like the most desirable woman on the planet?

"Okay," I say, and I think everyone in the room is shocked when I stand up and proceed to sit down in front of Ryder's spread thighs before removing the elastic from my hair.

His legs tighten around me, and his fingers slide through the strands before immediately getting caught up in a knot. "I'll go get a brush," he whispers in my ear, his lips brushing against my lobe.

The hairs on my arms stand on end.

What the hell am I doing? I'm playing with fire. Ryder is dangerous and I know it. He's an asshole who uses women. If my best friend's own words hadn't been warning enough, I had now seen the proof with my own eyes.

Womanizer.

Over-confident egomaniac.

"I have a brush in my purse," Kenzie says, reaching beside the couch. She tosses a brush on Ryder's lap, doing her best to hide her smile.

She fails miserably. Deklan does, too, as they both watch us.

"Scoot back," Ryder says, one hand on my shoulder, pulling me against him as he sits forward in the chair.

My upper back and lower neck is wedged against his junk, and he makes no effort to shift or change position.

Every nerve in my body is on edge.

To my enormous relief, he moves back.

I expect him to have the skills of a five year-old and am

stunned when instead he slowly and meticulously brushes out the knots from my hair for five of the longest minutes of my life.

I won't lie. It feels amazing. My eyes are feeling heavy. Even as a kid, I loved it when my mom brushed my hair. It was one sure way for her to get me to settle down and get ready for bed.

His long fingers separate my hair into three sections.

He's actually going to braid my hair. I unconsciously hold my breath.

Does he intentionally keep touching my neck? Was it on purpose?

Ryder starts braiding my hair, and I can tell he's done this before. He moves slowly, one hand stopping to hold the braid in one hand while he slides the fingers of his left hand over the side of my head.

I stare at the TV but I see nothing.

I'm a bundle of emotions and feelings as his fingers brush my neck time and again.

This was such a bad idea…

Why am I suddenly so aware of everything about him? Of his scent, of the way his feet are tucked up right against my sides. The scent of him that is both an earthy smell and a sporty scent that makes my pulse quicken.

"Let me see that hair tie," he finally says and I hand him the elastic band, nearly jumping when his hand lingers on mine.

It's in those few pulse pounding moments that I recall where those hands have been and I nearly drop the elastic band before he can grab it.

I will definitely be showering and scrubbing my hair when I get back to Kenzie's.

"Done," he says, sounding far too pleased with himself.

I reach back and feel the tight braid.

"Wow, who knew you had such skills, Ryder?" Kenzie remarks, and she and Deklan share a laugh.

"What can I say? My babysitter used to ask me to braid her hair."

Kenzie's brows lift and I can tell her mind has gone the same place mine has. I can't quite see Ryder braiding a babysitter's hair.

I stand and walk to the bathroom, secretly wondering if he's done something that makes me look like an idiot.

I check the braid out in the mirror.

Not bad. In fact, I'm actually really impressed. I debate taking the braid out, but decide he made the effort...and I have a point to prove, right?

I take a few minutes and when I walk out, Ryder is snoring in the chair.

"Maybe we should go so he can crash," I say, never so ready to leave a place in my life.

Kenzie agrees. "Yeah, it's late and I don't need mom on my ass."

Deklan looks disappointed, and once again I feel a little awkward for being the proverbial third wheel. Now I realize how Ryder must have felt all this time.

"Come on," Deklan says to Ryder, nudging his shoulder.

Ryder looks over at him through slitted eyes.

"Dude, just leave me here."

Deklan is vacillating whether to leave him alone or to bring him. I actually feel kind of sorry for the guy. He's so devoted to keeping his best friend off drugs. He shouldn't have to play babysitter twenty-four seven.

Kenzie threads her fingers through Deklan's. "He's tired. Let him sleep."

"You want us to help pull the bed out for you?" Deklan asks, already moving to do it for him.

"Dude," Ryder says. "I can manage. Quit acting like my dad."

Deklan actually looks likes he has been smacked across the face.

I'm hiding a smile as Kenzie meets my gaze.

Ryder gives me a salute. "See you later, ladies."

I mutter a goodbye and soon we're in Deklan's truck heading for Kenzie's house.

"He'll be fine," Kenzie says, doing her best to reassure him. "He just had an off night. Everyone does. He's human."

"It's not that," Deklan says, brushing a hand over his jaw. "I mean, we all have nights where we're not feeling it. He managed. It's Terry. He doesn't like me leaving Ryder alone at the house. He's mentioned it to me a few times, so the last thing I need is him getting on my case about it."

I knew Terry was Curtis's older brother and the owner of the house.

"Ryder is probably already asleep anyway. It's not like he's roaming the house. Plus, Brooke and Curtis are there."

Deklan glances at me. "Yeah, that's true. And we're moving out anyway."

"Moving?" It's clear by Kenzie's reaction and the tone of her voice that she's surprised by the news.

"Uncle Steve said I could rent the apartment above the shop. It seemed like the right thing to do, especially given the fact that Terry is getting burned out with the band. He wants his basement back, and I don't blame him. I would too.

"I thought Ryder was staying with you temporarily." Kenzie sits up straighter. "You said that once he had a few drug-free weeks under his belt that he'd be going home soon."

Deklan runs a hand through his dark hair, his long bangs hanging over his left eye. "His mom doesn't want him home. His dad has tried to sway her, but she's not having it. He doesn't need her judgment right now when he's doing so well."

Kenzie had told me about Ryder's mom throwing him out. At the time I hadn't felt bad for him, but now I sort of did.

"I want my own place anyway. It's been nice living with

Curtis and Terry, and I've saved a lot these past years, but I'm ready. Plus, Steve's giving us a great break on the price in exchange for keeping an eye on the place. You know, security."

"And you just have to walk downstairs to go to work," I add. I get a sidelong glance and an elbow in the ribs from Kenzie for my trouble.

She's pissed, and I know all about her concerns. She'd told me what she thinks about most of the girls who hang out at *Branded*. Deklan has created his own following during the years, and his easygoing manner seems to draw people in even more. He's easy to talk to, easy to be around, and let's face it—extremely easy on the eyes.

Deklan grins at me. "Exactly. See, babe...your best friend thinks it's a good idea, so it can't be too bad."

I'm sure the thought of having Ryder constantly underfoot is far from appealing to Kenzie, especially in the foreseeable future. I don't blame her, and yet I respect Deklan and his love for the man he considers a brother. He's devoted to taking care of him.

"When will you be moving?"

"First of August."

"So a little over a week?" Her voice is incredulous.

Deklan nods.

The hand that had been on Deklan's thigh is now back on her lap.

He puts his hand on her thigh and she straightens her shoulders. At least she doesn't remove his hand from her leg.

Personally, I think she's been a complete saint, especially since she still hangs around the guy who was originally her boyfriend but cheated on her. In this case, she didn't have a choice. Deklan wasn't going to leave his friend high and dry, period. She needed to get onboard and fast, because I was pretty certain he wouldn't be changing his mind.

"Is he going to actually work?" she asks, obviously looking for anything to justify her anger. "As in a real job?"

The nerve in Deklan's jaw tics. "He's been helping me around the shop, and Uncle Steve said Ryder can work the front desk."

"What about Phyllis?" Kenzie crosses her arms over her chest. "I thought she worked the front desk?"

"She works part-time, and Ryder will work part-time. Maybe he'll start school in September. I'd love to see him go to Clark. Maybe he could get his Associates, and then he can move to WSU. Who knows, maybe you'll be going to college together."

"Are you paying for that, too?" Kenzie says, the sarcasm dripping from her voice.

I looked out the window, feeling a huge fight coming on. I knew better than to try and help ease the tension. When Kenzie got something on her mind, it took a while for her to work through it. Hopefully Deklan knew that by now.

Releasing a heavy sigh, Deklan removes his hand from her thigh and puts it on the stick shift.

"He's my brother, Kenzie. I won't leave him to fend for himself. I'm sorry, but I can't do it."

"But you'll uproot your entire life for him. You told me not that long ago that you were saving for a house that you've been eyeing since you were a kid."

"And I'll get that house…one day."

I roll down the window and both of them go quiet on me.

The second he pulls into the driveway and comes to a stop, I open the door and get out.

Kenzie is right behind me.

"Babe…" Deklan sounds exasperated.

"Talk to him," I say, stopping short, causing her to run into my back.

I'm relieved when she turns back to him.

I climb the stairs to the apartment and thankfully the door is unlocked. Cole is sitting on his hide-a-bed wearing pajama bottoms and nothing else.

My breath catches in my throat.

"You barely made curfew," Cole says, lifting a soda to his lips.

I try not to stare at his six-pack but fail miserably. "Yeah, barely. Is your mom up?"

"I'm not sure. She went to bed about an hour ago."

I hesitate, hoping Kenzie would walk in. "Kenzie is saying good night to Deklan."

He nods. "That could take a while."

"Yeah." I smile, wishing I didn't feel so awkward around him. "Well, good night."

Cole frowns at me. "Not so fast." He pats the space beside him. "Come on, watch a movie with me."

"Okay."

My voice comes out a little strangled.

"You want to get your pajamas on first?" The interest I see in his eyes is unmistakable.

I glance at the door, expecting Kenzie to walk in any second.

"Yeah," I say, and head toward Kenzie's room.

EIGHT

A nge

Oh my God!

My stomach tightens with excitement. Cole wants to hang out with me. Melissa's door is closed and the light is off. I'm trying not to get too excited, but as I take off my clothes and put them in the hamper beside the door, I remember every night I had lain awake wondering what it would be like to be with Cole.

I put on a cute cami and boxers combo and apply lip gloss before I walk back to the living room. For a second I consider taking down the braid but decide at the last minute to leave it.

Cole gives me a sidelong glance.

"What did you guys do today?" he asks, and I take a seat beside him on the hide-a-bed. I want to go back and put my sweater on as the blast of cool air from the window air-conditioner hits my skin. My nipples pebble against my bra and I know the headlights are on because Cole's gaze abruptly shifts to my chest. He stares so long, I am half tempted to cross my arms.

So embarrassing...

"*The Frozen* had a concert," I say, relieved when his gaze meets mine.

"Are they any good?" he asks, sounding kind of bored.

"They're amazing. Your cousin has an incredible voice. You should come hear them sometime."

I wonder if he's heard anything I said. His gaze is shifting slowly over my body. "Maybe I will."

Okay then, I guess he *is* listening.

Kenzie walks in a second later and the door slams shut behind her. Oh no. She barely glances at us as she marches by.

"I better go check to make sure she's okay." I'm a bit surprised she's so mad that Ryder is moving in with Deklan. She has a year of high school to finish, so it's not like she'd be moving in with him. That, or she just really wanted him to save for his dream house. Either way, I empathized with her. It couldn't be easy to have to share your boyfriend with his best friend.

Or had she hoped he would ask her to move in? It's not like she's the first high school girl to move in with her boyfriend before graduation. My mother would never allow it, and the old Melissa wouldn't have gone for it...but the new Melissa might feel differently.

Before I can take a step, Cole reaches out and grabs my hand. "Trouble in paradise?"

His hand is warm, and strangely, I find myself comparing those long fingers to Ryder's. Ryder's fingers were also long, like Cole's. For some reason, I couldn't imagine Cole braiding my hair.

But then again, stranger things have happened.

Then I remember where Ryder's fingers had been earlier

tonight, and the look on his face as he'd left the janitor's closet, still adjusting his clothes after messing around with the slutty brunette.

I really do need to take a shower tonight and wash my hair.

"They're fine. Just fighting over Ryder."

Cole snorts. "That guy's a real winner." His voice drips with sarcasm.

"Yeah, he's something alright."

"I can't believe Kenzie dated that loser."

I wouldn't go so far as to call Ryder a loser. I mean, yes, he did struggle with drugs, but apparently he hadn't been the only one in the band to do so. I nearly reminded him about his own cousin who had overdosed a few months ago, but refrained.

"They should boot his ass out of the band."

Ryder did have God-given talent, and the boy could work a crowd. "He's Deklan's best friend…so that's probably not going to happen."

"They did it once. They can do it again."

"True," I say, surprised I'm a bit defensive of Ryder. That, or maybe I was tired of talking about Ryder. Plus, I wanted to know more about Cole's college life, and since he wasn't being too forthcoming, I thought I'd ask a few questions. "How about you? Are you dating anyone?"

His brows furrow as though it's the stupidest question he's ever heard. "Football doesn't really give me time to date."

I'm thrilled by the news. "Football's not year-round, is it?"

The corners of his mouth twitch. "No, but I train year-round."

It's my turn to frown. "Why?"

"Hey, what can I say…I'm an active guy."

I knew that. Cole has always taken care of his body. I recall the comments about his body being a temple. Kenzie told me about the smoking hot remark about the good-looking girls at UW, too. The handsome quarterback would obviously have his share of women.

"What about you, Ange? You have a boyfriend?"

I rarely blushed. Being the head of the yearbook committee and someone who was always comfortable speaking to groups, I was used to having attention directed at me. I *liked* having that attention directed at me and I always delivered what I had to say with confidence, and yet I suddenly found it extremely difficult to put two words together. "No, I don't have a boyfriend." I wonder if it's possible that he doesn't know I had lusted after him for years before he left for college. I'd been at his house practically every single day. And he'd treated me like his little sister's best friend. Some days he acknowledged me with a 'hey, Ange.' Other days it was a nod. Sometimes there was no acknowledgement at all.

"Any guy would be lucky to have you."

"What a nice thing to say."

"I mean it," he says, rotating his shoulder in a forward motion and wincing. "I was playing catch today and I think I pulled a muscle. Would you mind rubbing it for me?"

Had he just asked me to rub him down? "Of course... but let me talk to your sister first. I want to make sure she's okay."

"Sure, go ahead. I'll be here waiting for you."

I walk down the hallway. The light in the bathroom was on and the door was slightly ajar. I knock once. "Kenz."

"Yeah." She opens the door. A washrag hangs from her right hand, and I swear she had tears in her eyes.

"You okay?"

She motions me in and I shut the door behind me.

"I'm so tired of Ryder. I know Deklan loves him and has this weird loyalty toward him. I do...but he just gets under my skin, you know?" She blows out an exasperated breath. "He is so frustrating."

"Is this more about the new apartment or—"

"I don't know. I mean, I trust Deklan. I do. But the thought of him having an apartment above the tattoo shop, and then sharing it with Ryder...it's too much. I thought the whole Ryder thing was temporary. Before, I was used to hanging out with him. Now I'm just sick of his face."

"Okay, so you trust Deklan...but you don't trust Ryder." I didn't state it as a question. It was common knowledge that Ryder slept with anyone and anything. He'd proven that just this very night.

"I don't trust him, Ange. Plus, girls already hang out at *Branded* just to see Deklan. He has groupies, and he's getting even more now that Ryder is there. What will they do when they realize he lives above the shop with Ryder? He wasn't even living at Curtis's before and he already had overnight guests. I'll have no control over who is there, and what if some random chick ends up spending the night and crawls into bed with Deklan?" Her voice is getting louder by the second.

"Kenz, let's take Ryder out of the equation for now. Deklan loves you. He's head over heels crazy about you. He watches you even when you don't realize it, and it's like he can't quite believe you belong to him."

A brow shoots up. "Really?"

"Really. He's not going to do anything to ruin your relationship. If he could, he would change this. He's just torn. He's in love with you, and he loves Ryder. Think about it—Ryder's family took him in when he didn't have anyone. Don't you think in a way that he's repaying the favor by taking Ryder in now, especially when Ryder's parents are pretty much finished with him?"

"True...but still, I had hoped when Deklan moved out that he would be alone. That we would finally have peace."

I nudge her. "You want your man to yourself, the white picket fence and all that. Yes, I get it. And I know how nice it will be to have your own place without Terry or Curtis. Especially since it must be said that Deklan is currently living in a freaking dungeon."

Kenzie laughs. "It's not a dungeon."

"Uh, yes it is. It's freaking depressing. Just think how great it will be to have a place that's not a practically windowless, airless basement with zero to little appeal. A downtown apartment on the second floor that overlooks the park. Now that doesn't suck."

"You're right. The apartment would have an insane view of the park."

I smile. "See, there are positives such as not having to label your food."

Kenzie had told me about Terry's obsession with labeling every single food item. She's caving. I can feel it.

"I bet he'll love having you help decorate the new place."

Her brows lift, and I can tell her mind's already racing. "Maybe tomorrow we can go to IKEA and pick up something for the new place."

"You mean like a peace offering for being such a whiner?"

She frowns. "I'm not a whiner."

"Yeah, you are. Just a little. But I think Deklan will love whatever you buy. Plus, he needs definite help in the interior design area. You do have your mother's good taste."

Her smile is even brighter now. "You think?"

"Um, I know."

Her phone rings and she grins. "It's Deklan."

I laugh. "He's probably still in the driveway."

She hits the answer button. "Hey."

Happy to have helped my friend, I pump some lotion into my hands. My hands are going to be soft, smooth, and ready to work some magic on Mr. Quarterback's amazing muscles.

"I know, me too, babe." Kenzie bites her thumbnail. "I was jealous at the thought of girls coming to your apartment. I know how women gravitate towards Ryder, and how he can't say no to anyone."

I can hear Deklan say he doesn't want anyone but her, and the declaration gives me goose bumps.

The two are so lucky, and I hope to have what my friend has. One day...I will.

"I know. That's exactly what Ange said." Kenzie gives me a wink.

I just scored big points with Deklan.

"I know. I love you, too." She laughs. "Yes, I swear."

I smile. All is right in the world once again, and now I can get back to my own love life.

"Kenz, I'm going to watch TV with Cole for a bit."

She gives me a hug, a kiss on the cheek, and whispers, "Thank you, Ange."

How I've missed those hugs, and it's times like these past few minutes that I hope we have more of before we both return to our respective schools for our senior year.

I give her a wink and walk back into the living room where Cole is now sitting in front of the wingback chair.

"Ready for me, huh?"

"Yep."

Cole doesn't move, and I'm forced to climb onto the chair in an unladylike fashion. My spread thighs rest on either side of his broad shoulders...and I'm reminded of how I had been sitting on the floor in front of Ryder earlier tonight.

He rests against me and I inhale. He smells like body spray. I want to bury my face in his hair and wrap my arms around his neck.

Of course I don't and I won't.

"My right trap is killing me." He squeezes the muscle with his hand to emphasize just how much it's hurting. The motion makes the shredded sinew flex beneath his golden skin and my mouth goes dry.

I'm incredibly motivated to help him be pain free. How many times in the past five years have I wished for a scenario just like this?

I push his hand aside and start working the muscle. He gives a satisfied grunt and I immediately gain confidence as the seconds tick by.

"Maybe a little bit of lotion would work well," he suggests, and my confidence goes down the toilet.

I wait for him to stand up and get the lotion, but when he doesn't make any effort to move, I jump up and rush to the bathroom that is now empty. I hear Kenzie's laughter coming from her room.

Grabbing the bottle off the bathroom counter, I make my way back to Cole, and I now have a skip in my step.

The lotion makes his skin more pliable and I'm able to feel the knotted muscles beneath my thumbs. Once or twice he even winces. I let up slightly and knead gently, working from the outside in.

I get a moan from him and I can't help but smile. I am incredibly focused until he winces.

Damn it! "Sorry."

"Don't be sorry," he says, glancing back at me, his green eyes flashing with an intensity that surprises me. His gaze shifts to my lips.

I swallow hard, and suddenly I feel like I'm completely out of my comfort zone.

"You've grown up, Ange." I hear the appreciative tone of his voice.

"I'll be eighteen in November."

"I know," he says, laughing under his breath. "I have to keep reminding myself that my little sister is a woman."

"Yep, and we grew up somewhere along the way."

He places a hand over one of mine and squeezes. "I'm so glad you're here. Kenzie really needs a friend. Brooke is fine and all, but she did lead her down a dangerous path. She needs someone who runs in a similar circle as you."

I wasn't ready to talk shit about anyone, especially a family member, but I am tempted because it's not like Brooke has been overly nice to me. Still, I'm wary to say anything just in case. "Brooke's good to Kenzie."

"No, I know. I'm just saying that she can be a bit intense and doesn't hang with the best crowd."

There it was again, the jab about Kenzie's group of friends.

"They're not all bad," I say with forced humor. "Plus, I'm sure you have a few friends that are questionable as well…or wait, are they all gorgeous jocks like you?"

Crap. The second the words came out of my mouth, I wish I could pull them back in.

"You think I'm gorgeous?" His teeth flash white.

Any regret about the outburst flees as he pulls my head down and his lips hover over mine. "You're so pretty," he whispers, seconds before he kisses me.

I start shaking. I can't freaking believe what is happening. I'm kissing Cole Parker.

I've waited for this moment for a lifetime.

His breath is hot, sweet, and minty. His tongue strokes mine, and not in a tentative, testing way…but in an 'I'm going to ravage you' kind of way.

When he breaks the kiss a minute later, he says, "I've wanted to do that since I saw you wearing that sexy sundress."

I need to pull out that sundress again.

That, or go to the mall and buy more sundresses. Hell, I'd buy one in every color.

He turns and is kneeling in front of me, his big hands on either one of my knees, and I savor the skin on skin contact.

As I stare at him, I'm reminded of a Greek God statue that has come to life. His chiseled body is flawless, his face amazing, and I want more than anything to bury my fingers in his curly golden hair.

Without a doubt, Cole Parker is my greatest fantasy come to life.

I lose all sense of control. I kiss him and slide my fingers through his golden curls.

Strong, callused fingers slide slowly up my thighs, to the part of me that is burning for him.

Holy shit. My heart is slamming so hard it reverberates in my ears.

Am I ready for this? I wonder, and as the excitement turns to trepidation I grab his wrists a second later.

Apparently I'm not quite ready.

His brows furrow, but only for a second as his hands continue their upward slide. His thumbs move downward, toward my crotch.

I grip his wrists tightly and forcefully push them aside.

I see the shock on his face. The frown as he sets back on his heels. That look says that he's disappointed and thinks I'm a tease.

Am I a tease? One second I'm rubbing his shoulders, the next I'm making out with him, and when he wants to take it further, I play coy.

"I'm sorry," I blurt, and then wish for the moment back again.

What an idiot. What am I thinking? I've wanted Cole for what seemed like a lifetime and now when he finally wants me back, I put the brakes on?

Hearing footsteps in the hallway, I jump to my feet.

So does Cole, who gathers enough wits to slide onto the hide-a-bed as though he's always been there since Kenzie first came home.

Kenzie is wearing pajama bottoms with stars and half moons and a well-worn baby blue t-shirt that I remember her telling me came from Deklan.

"How did the phone call go?" I ask, even though I already know. I hope she doesn't see my heated cheeks.

Taking a seat on the edge of the hide-a-bed, she glances over at me. "Good. Thank you for talking some sense into me."

"That's what friends are for."

She glances at her brother and frowns. "Don't you own

a shirt?"

"Ange was rubbing my shoulders for me. I had a kink."

Her brows lift. "Using my buddy as a massage therapist isn't cool."

"I don't mind," I say, and bite my lip when she gives me a strange look.

"Alrighty then. Well, I'm going to crash."

I jump up and stretch. "It's been a long day."

Cole is watching me. He doesn't want me to go.

Kenzie is watching me, too.

This is too awkward. "Good night, Cole," I say as I start toward the room.

"Wait, I'm getting a glass of water first." Kenzie walks into the kitchen.

"You sure you don't want to watch a movie with me?" Cole asks, and I know the question is directed at me.

"You can stay up," Kenzie says while filling a glass with water.

"No, I'm completely burned out. I'll be asleep before my head hits the pillow." I was such a liar. I'd probably toss and turn all night wondering what Cole was doing or thinking.

I feel so strange. Where is the elation I should be experiencing right now? Why do I instead feel trepidation all of the sudden? Is it just because I'm all too aware of my inexperience and never really figured I would be in this position with the man I desired? Or is it because a certain dark-haired, blue-eyed rocker made me feel sensations when he'd been doing something as simple as braiding my hair that had me thinking that maybe I wasn't quite sure what, or who, I wanted?

NINE

R^{yder}

I slide the pills into my pocket and hand the guy fifty bucks before I start back up the street toward *Branded*.

I had told Deklan I was leaving to pick up some lunch for us, so I make sure I stop by a sandwich joint and grab a couple of subs before heading back to the shop.

It's only been twenty-four hours since I had taken the Vicodin, and I'm excited as I slip an Oxy into my mouth. I had slept like a rock last night and savored the full night's sleep—something that hadn't happened since I'd stopped using.

I wouldn't get carried away. I just needed a few days to catch up on sleep, I told myself, wondering if I should slip into the grocery store and pick up a razor blade to cut up the remaining pills. Snorting is so much more effective than swallowing. I decide against it. I can't run the risk of Deklan finding a razor blade among my things, and knowing him, he'd find it.

I suck on the pill for a minute and then crush it with my back teeth, using my tongue to dislodge the rest.

Hopefully Deklan would continue to be preoccupied with his woman issues. Last night when he'd returned from taking Kenzie and Ange home, he'd gone straight to his room. I could hear him on the phone and could tell by the tone of his voice that the conversation had been intense. Well, at least for a while. Soon his mood changed from dark and brooding to laughing at everything she said.

Even if things weren't going well in paradise, I still needed to be careful and watch myself. I couldn't afford to get sloppy.

The boy watched everything, and he was watching me closely last night. I'd had to use a distraction and braid Ange's hair. Trust me, I'd rather pull that hair than braid it, but I couldn't resist after her smartass mouth. That girl could give as good as she gave.

I wonder, and not for the first time, what she'd be like between the sheets.

Speak of the devil, I think at the sight of Kenzie's car parked in front of the shop.

I walk into *Branded* and Ange is sitting on the Victorian fainting couch leafing through one of the many magazines that Phyllis has bought. She's wearing a bikini top beneath a razorback black and white striped tank and surprisingly short black cotton shorts. It's normally not Ange's style to show off too much, but I like that she's revealing more of those killer legs. Her body is tight and toned.

"You getting a tattoo?" I ask.

She looks up in surprise and shakes her head. "Not today."

Wow, no smartass quip?

A hint of a smile tugs at her lips. It's like the girl can read my mind.

No Kenzie or Deklan in sight, which means they must have escaped to the break room, or what we called Uncle Steve's office.

"So what are you up to today?" I ask. She wore absolutely no makeup and I thought she looked amazing.

"We're headed to the lake."

"Merwin?" I ask. I wish we were going to the lake. I was locked into working on a sunny Sunday afternoon while Deklan inked a grandma who was celebrating her sixty-third birthday with a new tattoo.

"Who else is going?"

"Brooke, Curtis...Cole."

I was surprised that Curtis hadn't mentioned it when we ate breakfast this morning, but then again, he isn't exactly the chatty type. "So jock boy is going, huh? You must be elated."

I regret the words the second I say them because she drops her gaze back to the magazine.

She clears her throat and looks at me. "Are you going?"

"That depends."

"On what?"

"Is Deklan going?"

"I imagine."

"Then that would be a yes."

"You two are joined at the hip." She's teasing and I really like this new Ange. That, or the drugs are just really starting to set in. Probably both.

"Not by my choice, trust me."

I wait for a flippant comment but she surprises me when she remains quiet. The attitude of late has been less hate and more tolerant.

Obviously she realizes that I'm on hostage status until Deklan relinquishes his hold.

The door opens and an older woman with an Elvis tattoo on her bicep enters.

"You must be Mrs. Easton, " I ask the lady, who is

grinning from ear to ear.

"Why, yes, young man, I am. Are you Deklan?"

"No, I'm Ryder. Have a seat next to this beautiful young lady and I'll get your artist for you."

Ange flashes Mrs. Easton a welcoming smile.

I walk through the spider-web gates that lead from the waiting area into the shop and down the hallway toward Steve's office. I don't bother knocking on the door before I enter.

Kenzie has her pert little ass on the desk, and Deklan is between her spread thighs. He has a hand down the front of her skimpy bottoms and it's clear what he's doing. Kenzie's hand is also moving in a certain motion and I freeze.

I don't blame him for banging his chick in the office. She's smoking hot in her barely there bikini, and from the second she walked into the store with a see-through cover-up, Deklan must have had a hard on.

I go to the bathroom and decide to drop back by the office later to inform him his client is ready.

Kenzie's soft whimpers mock me through the thin walls. An image of what I'd just seen burns in my mind and I can't help but think of Ange in her short shorts.

I unbuckle my pants and slide my hand around my cock.

My head falls back on my shoulders and I imagine what Ange looks like without her clothes on. Long seconds drag into minutes. The drugs are apparently starting to work because I can't get my dick hard to save my life. I give it another minute, but it's no use.

Disgusted, I avoid my reflection in the gothic mirror above the sink and wash my hands before I walk back to the office.

I knock on the door with a few obnoxiously loud raps and count silently to ten before pushing the door open.

They haven't moved, though Deklan's hands are nowhere near her crotch. In fact, Kenzie moves back and presses her legs together.

I clear my throat and Deklan looks up at me, irritation clear in his eyes.

I set the bag on the desk and remove my sandwich. "Your client is here."

A nerve in his jaw tics. "Cool. I'll be right there."

Kenzie slides off the desk. Her cheeks are flushed and her golden tanned body is smoking hot in the nearly transparent material of the cover-up.

My friend is the luckiest motherfucker on the planet.

And I am the stupidest son of a bitch, I remind myself. I had that…and I let it slip right through my fingers.

"Headed to the lake today, huh?" I say, probably staring a little longer at her firm body than I should.

"Yeah, I'm meeting my brother there," she says, her fingers weaving through Deklan's. "Brooke and Curtis said they might join us later. Are you guys coming by?"

"We'll definitely be there," Deklan says, his gaze skipping over her body. I know my friend. He has the world's best poker face, but he's worried. He doesn't like to share and he doesn't like guys looking at his woman.

Looks like he's shit out of luck today, because there's not a guy alive who won't be staring at her.

"By the way, Dek, I just booked you another appointment after this one."

Deklan scowls at me. "I hope you got a number, because you'll have to cancel."

I crack a smile. "I'm just fuckin' with you. I can tell you don't want to be here. In fact, you're already at the lake with your smokin' hot girlfriend."

"Dude, you're not helping," Deklan says, pulling Kenzie close and giving her a long kiss that makes her sigh.

I've heard those throaty moans of hers coming from Deklan's room at night. That's another reason I'm looking forward to the apartment. There is a bathroom and a utility room between my room and his, which means I don't need to hear the nightly sex rounds of sighs and moans.

"I'd better get going. I told Cole I'd be there by now." Kenzie is walking toward the door, and Deklan's eyes are glued to her high, tight ass.

I know the gleam in her eye. She's enjoying the power she has over my friend. I get it. Chicks know the power of the vagina. They use it at will.

I fall in step behind Kenzie, and Deklan shoves me out of the way and gives me a warning glare.

"You're so screwed," I say under my breath.

Ange

I won't lie. I'm relieved that I'm getting a few hours of quality time with Kenzie before the boys arrive at the lake. I have my best friend all to myself ... at least until later this afternoon before Brooke and her boyfriend show up.

I love the band. I do. I enjoy their practices, but seriously I am so ready to do something other than have my social life revolve around *The Frozen's* band practice and concerts.

"What are you thinking?"

I glance up at Kenzie. Her blonde hair is in a sloppy bun and she has on the cutest hot pink two-piece and sheer cover-up. She's always been a natural beauty—and I think she was gorgeous just the way she was now—with just a little mascara and lip gloss. She's adorable, and I had loved the way that Deklan was freaking out. His mouth had dropped open when we walked in. Kenzie had surprised me when she'd taken him by the hand and led him to the backroom to tell him something. No doubt to make sure they were fine after last night's blowout. They'd walked out of the office with cheeks flushed and smiles on their faces, so I didn't have to wonder what exactly they had talked about. "I'm thinking about how much fun I'm having here."

She grins. "I'm glad you're here, Ange. I don't want you to go back to California."

I was glad, too. I wasn't at all homesick for my family. I loved my sisters, but being stuck with them in the Hawaiian timeshare wasn't my idea of paradise. My parents were a bit on the conservative side, although my mom was a realist—hence the sexual education talk just days after getting my period.

My mom and I had always been close. Lately, she had been getting on my nerves though with her constant yammering about me attending Pepperdine. Pepperdine was Mom's alma mater, so in her mind I basically had no choice.

Although my father tells me differently.

Mom wins all the battles though.

Always had, always will.

Kenzie pulls onto a paved driveway that weaves through the trees.

I put the visor down, apply some lip gloss, and tie the strings of my bikini a little tighter, hiking the girls a bit higher. I had gone for a solid black bikini.

I hope Cole liked it.

Ryder sure seemed to…damn it. Why was I thinking about him again? This morning when I had seen him at the shop, I had been reminded of him braiding my hair and how he'd come to mind when Cole had kissed me.

Liking Ryder would be a huge mistake. He's the kind of guy who could get me in hot water right away. The saying *'hit it and quit it'* came to mind, and yet how was I so sure that Cole wouldn't be the same way?

Well…because he was my Cole. But that Cole had tried to do more than kiss me, so maybe I didn't know him so well after all.

Kenzie chatters away. I can't focus on anything. The lake is packed with people. With a blanket tucked under one arm and a small cooler full of bottled water and snacks in the other, I scan the sandy beach that is littered with families for Cole. There are a good number of trees just beyond the sand. All the shade is taken. "I'll text Cole."

Seconds later, her phone rings that she has a text message. Kenzie glances over her shoulder to the left.

Cole is already walking our way. Beside him is a stocky guy-next-door blond and a gorgeous girl with stick straight brown hair and the longest legs I've ever seen. Her hipbones are razor sharp.

Girlfriend needs to eat a cheeseburger, stat.

My stomach drops to my toes. And here I had been feeling kind of confident.

I wonder if she's with the cute blond but lose hope when the girl with the endless legs gives Cole a little love pat on the ass.

I nearly drop the cooler.

Kenzie glances at me, obviously to check and see if I'd noticed.

I'd noticed all right. My stomach is already in a knot.

What about the kiss we had shared just last night? Had that meant nothing?

Was he pissed that I'd stopped him from going further? That, or he'd gotten a little too close to little sis's friend and now he was backpedaling…

Cole doesn't even glance back at her though. He smiles and reaches out to me. I realize almost too late that he wants the cooler.

I want to hurl it at him.

He knows it too, I think, because he avoids eye contact.

I'm glad I have my sunglasses on. I don't want him to see that I'm hurt in any way.

Or maybe I'm just reading too much into that little slap-happy tap on the ass.

Introductions are made. Leggy is Nadia and she has a very faint Ukranian accent.

Nadia reaches for Cole's hand. She's grinning from ear-to-ear at Kenzie. Apparently she knows Kenzie and Cole are related. She manages a quick glance at me and a polite head-nod before returning her full attention to Kenzie.

I walk behind the others and hate that I have to take one-and-a-half steps for every single step that Nadia takes.

There's an open field with lush green grass littered with a dozen oak trees where older couples and families with small children sit on chairs and lay on blankets.

We pick a spot with no shade in sight and drop our blankets.

Cole immediately joins a volleyball game in progress, while Nadia plops her skinny butt beside a group of girls who are cheering on the guys playing. Typical guys—they're checking us out pretty hard, but I can tell that Cole reminds them that we're family because they laugh and focus on the game.

Kenzie takes off her cover-up and I remove my shorts and tank top. I take my time putting on sunblock, soaking in the beautiful lake and the surrounding area where picnic tables are sitting amongst evergreen trees.

I can see why Washington has grown on Kenzie. It might rain a lot, but the greenery was unlike anything I had ever seen.

"Will you put some of that on my back?" Kenzie rolls onto her stomach.

I squirt lotion into my hand. I can feel eyes on us and decide to slow my movements, taking my time working the lotion into Kenzie's legs and lower back. When I ease my fingers under her bikini string, one of the guys hits another.

I press my lips together to keep from smiling. Men. They are so predictable.

Kenzie grins but says nothing. She knows me better than I know myself sometimes.

Cole's team scores, and when he looks our way, he barks at one of the guys.

Obviously big brother isn't enjoying the show as much

as his buddies are.

Kenzie snorts under her breath.

I set the lotion aside and lie on my back and close my eyes.

"You want me to put lotion on you?" Kenzie asks and laughs wickedly.

"I'm sure the boys would love that." I grin. "Maybe when I flip over. I've got my front covered."

I watch the game under lowered lids as the sun's rays tan my skin.

Kenzie's phone signals she has a text.

She glances at it and smiles.

"Your man?"

"Yes." She eases up on to her elbows. "He's checking to make sure we arrived."

Yeah, right. He wanted to make sure she was being good and not forgetting that she had a hotter than sin boyfriend. "Be sure to tell him that we're hanging out with your brother and eight of his closest ultra-ripped friends, watching them play volleyball."

"I'm not watching the guys though," she says, as though she's trying to convince me.

"Yeah, but they're watching you."

I take a picture of Kenzie and post it on my social networking site. Ryder is my friend. I know Deklan doesn't have a page or like social networking, but Ryder does. I smile to myself, and I know that part of the reason I posted the picture is because I know Deklan will hurry his ass here, which means Ryder will be with him.

I'd like to prove to Cole that he's not the only one who can attract the opposite sex. Maybe he's just trying to prove to me that there are other girls who will obviously go further with him than just kissing.

I watch the game, and more notably, Cole, who is tanned a golden brown. He's completely into the competition of the game. His gaze doesn't waver from the ball. The boy is focused. I could be naked on the sidelines and he probably wouldn't look.

"Game point," he yells as he serves the ball and runs up toward the net.

"Hey you," Brooke says, dropping her bag beside us.

Curtis is following a few steps behind with a couple of air mattresses tucked under one arm and a small cooler in the other. His blond dreadlocks are held up in a high pony. He has a nice face and amazing eyes under all that hair.

Brooke notices my gaze linger on her man and she frowns at me. "Hands off the goods, Ange."

I hold my hands, palms out. "Will do."

For the first time, she gives me a soft smile and I wonder if she's warming up to me after all.

My attention instantly returns to the game just as Cole spikes the ball down, nearly hitting his opponent on the head.

Finally, his gaze turns toward us. His grin is at once triumphant and cocksure. My pulse quickens as I realize he's looking straight at me, like he's almost demanding my attention.

From the corner of my eye, I can tell that Nadia is bristling at the attention Cole is showing me.

Elated, I smile back at him.

TEN

R^{yder}

"She's not answering."

Deklan is chewing away on his lip ring. The boy is nervous and it's not pretty to watch. I almost want to hand him one of the Xanax's in my pocket. I slipped another one while he wasn't watching and it's working its magic. Combined with the Oxy, I am floating and all my problems have mysteriously faded away into oblivion.

Even the guilt of using again has gone by the wayside. Today, I'm going to enjoy myself. Tomorrow is a new day. I'll stop using then.

"Maybe she left with her brother and his buddies," Deklan says, and I hate that he's become such a fucking pussy when it comes to this woman. Seriously, what the hell was the matter with him?

"An hour ago she was sunbathing with Ange and

hanging with her brother. Maybe she's gone for a swim. Think about it. It's not like she's going to take her phone into the water with her."

He nods, but he doesn't look any less worried.

"And two hours before that you were getting busy in Uncle Steve's office, so I'm seriously doubting she's on her back on someone else's desk."

Usually he would grin at that, but now he brushes a hand through his dark hair. He'd just finished with Mrs. Easton's tattoo, and all we had to do was clean his station before we left. "Her brother has friends. Like friends who are fellow athletes."

Deklan had an insane body for someone who wasn't into working out. Genetics had been kind to him, and he never met a punching bag he didn't like. I can't help it. I laugh. "Seriously, bro, your woman is crazy for you. You may not see it, but I do."

The sides of his mouth lift. "I trust her…it's just that I don't trust other guys. And we had our first real fight last night. Like she was seriously pissed off."

"Fight—about what?"

He hesitated, so I immediately know the argument had been about me.

"You should trust her, dude. She's crazy in love with you. It's like there's no other guy in the room when you're there."

"You think so?"

"I know it. So let's get out of here already."

Within fifteen minutes we had switched on the CLOSED sign at *Branded* and we're heading down the freeway toward the lake. Deklan had grown quiet, glancing at his phone every few seconds to see if he'd missed a call.

I check my phone as well and see the notices about Ange's post. There's pictures of a sunbathing Kenzie, and I have to say, the pics are extremely flattering. She looks amazing and there are already a good twenty comments that say the same thing, the majority from blond-haired surfer types who say they miss the gorgeous Parker girl.

"Well, I have the answer. This pic was taken a few minutes ago and she's sunbathing."

He grabs the phone and practically swerves off the road.

"Dude," I say, and snatch the phone out of his hand before we get into a wreck.

"Fuck," he says under his breath, while running a hand down his face.

"So what's it like?" I ask.

Deklan frowns. "What do you mean?"

"What's it like to really love someone? To be so into them that you can't focus on shit."

I have to wonder if he thinks I'm talking about someone else, because he looks confused. "Seriously? Am I really that bad?"

"Dude…"

He shrugs and releases a long sigh. "It's incredible. I just want to be with her all the time. Don't get me wrong—I like hanging with you and the guys. Kenzie just makes me feel like a better person."

"I get it." I laugh under my breath. The drugs have me in a relaxed state, and I have the insane urge to crack up over nothing, but this is not the time, especially when I'm having a rare heart-to-heart talk with my best friend.

"Do you think you'll marry her?" I'm being a complete smartass.

"Definitely…one day."

I thought he'd look at me and smirk or ask me if I was serious because Kenzie still has another year of high school left. Deklan always was the monogamous type when it came to his steady girlfriends.

"She's mine," he says, and there's no mistaking the possessiveness in his voice. "I feel protective of her, and I just want to be everything she wants."

"I think it's safe to say she feels the same."

"You really think so?"

"You're blind if you don't see it." I stare out at the passing landscape, wishing I had an ice-cold beer to alleviate my cottonmouth. I feel a flash of sadness come over me. Deklan has found someone he wants to be with forever. I wonder if I will ever have that. It must be incredible to be able to look into the future and already know what it is you want. I wonder if I will ever feel that way, or if I will always be alone.

Ange

I'm glad Curtis thought to bring an air mattress and was nice enough to offer it to me. Floating around a lake had to be one of the most incredible ways to pass an afternoon. Plus, it was a nice reprieve from having to listen to Nadia clap and bounce up and down every single time Cole or his team made a point.

I think girls have a sixth sense when it came to competition. We all knew what the other one was thinking, and therefore it made it easier to piss the other one off. Nadia had gotten under my skin and she knew it. Every time I glanced her way, she seemed to make an effort to flirt even more outrageously with Cole.

The trick was pretending like you didn't give a shit when really, it bothered the hell out of you.

Although Brooke drove me a bit crazy at times, I was grateful for the comedic intervention she provided. She had a way of talking shit about other girls that made me laugh, and pretty much put into words what I'd been thinking. Just having her around us made me feel protected too.

Brooke had immediately picked up on Nadia's overenthusiastic cheering of Cole.

Kenzie had to tell her to be quiet a few times, but Brooke just ignored her. Curtis said very little, but I noticed about every ten minutes or so he'd walk over to the shade of a tree and smoke a cigarette. He had been thrilled when we decided to hit the water.

I glance over at the dock where Kenzie is hanging out with Brooke and Curtis, along with at least a dozen other people. The three pre-pubescent boys that are doing cannonballs off the side of the dock are driving me bat-shit, and I wonder where the hell their parents are when, yet again, water from their jump sprays me.

I wade further away and watch a water-skier on the opposite side of the log pilings that keep boats and jet skis away from those of us in the bay. The wake sends me and the air mattress floating even further away from the dock.

Brooke and Kenzie laugh and I wonder if it's at my expense.

I need to get over my jealousy there. I know I'm a bit territorial when I'm around Brooke and Kenzie, and it makes me feel a bit manic.

For so many years I was used to it being just me and Kenzie and not having to share her with anyone else. We had other friends, granted, but no one took the place of Kenzie, and I had a feeling she felt the same way toward me. No one ever wanted to feel like the odd man out.

The water lulls me into a relaxing mode. I need to focus on all that is going right in my life and not what's going wrong. I'm in Washington and I have freedom from my parents and my sisters, which is amazing. And most of all, I'm with my best friend.

Plus, the guy of my dreams is home on summer break and living under the same roof. He'd kissed me, and I liked it, but my reaction to his touch made me seriously consider if I was ready to give up my virginity just yet. I just need to know if he wants more or if he is turned off because of me pulling away the other night.

I can't help but wonder about Nadia. Had he just met her, or had he met her during his previous visits to

Vancouver?

Guys like Cole expect a girl to put out, period. I'm sure in college he had a different girl in his bed every night. Hell, in high school I'd heard the stories about his many conquests and had seen him in action at the after game bonfires on the beach. The guy had skills and I had watched from a distance, wishing and hoping I had been the girl he was with.

Now I had the chance.

I glance toward the beach. The restrooms are blocking the view of Cole and his friends, which is probably a good thing. By now Nadia has no doubt joined the game and has all the men in the vicinity panting after her five foot nine inches of skinny bitch.

My gaze shifts to two dark-haired guys walking down the beach. They're impossible to miss, and there's not one girl, except for the chick glued to her tablet, who does not look their way.

Apparently I'm not immune either, because my pulse skitters.

Deklan and Ryder.

Ryder's board shorts are black and white and hanging low on his waist. The new tattoo is on his upper right bicep, and it looks good. It fits him. I imagine in a few years he'll be covered in ink just like his best friend.

Deklan is wearing blue board shorts and he's peeling off the wife-beater and staring at the direction of the dock.

My mouth goes a little dry.

I have to give it to my girl. Her man is shredded. I don't think I've ever met another guy with Deklan's musculature.

Lucky bastard.

He waves and Kenzie, Brooke, and Curtis wave back.

Ryder and Deklan leave their shirts, sandals, and belongings on the beach. Ryder talks to an older woman with three kids, who is nodding at something he says. I'm guessing that he's asking her to look after their things.

Deklan is already wading into the water and then dives

under. Ryder is right behind him.

I'm torn between wading over to the dock and joining them, or pretending to be sunbathing on my little air mattress.

Not wanting to seem desperate in any way, I opt to stay on the air mattress.

I watch as the two men swim toward the dock. Deklan gets there first and pulls himself up and onto the dock in one fluid motion. The girls on the dock are all atwitter as they take in his ripped, tattooed body dripping with water. Kenzie doesn't notice the other girls. Why should she when her dripping wet boyfriend leans down and gives her a thorough kissing? It's the sexiest thing I've ever seen, and I admit that I feel jealous of my friend and her relationship. How awesome would it be to have a man that is bat-shit crazy over you? I could only hope that one day I would find out for myself.

My gaze shifts to Ryder, who is holding onto the dock ladder with one hand. He's talking to the group. I smirk to myself. He apparently doesn't have the same upper body strength as his friend.

That, or he just wants to stay in the water.

Brooke points right at me. He turns and immediately starts swimming in my direction.

My throat grows so tight I can barely swallow.

With every strong stroke that brings him closer, I want to leap off the air mattress and swim as hard and as far as I can in the opposite direction.

Why does he have the ability to get under my skin like no one else?

Seconds later, he comes out of the water and whips his hair back.

With his hair slicked back you get a good look at that killer face, and I hate to say, I'm completely affected by it.

He's freaking perfect.

Damn him.

Even his teeth are straight and bright white.

"You look hot, Ange."

"Tha—" I stop short of telling him thanks, because I realize he's not meaning I look hot, as in incredible, but as in hot…like I'm melting, and he'd be right. I'm a California girl, but I'm used to a little bit of wind with my sun, and there's not a breeze in sight.

And I could use one right now.

It's definitely not helping that Ryder has a way of looking at me as though he can see right through the layers of my clothes.

He's wading in the water, and when he reaches up and holds onto the raft, he splashes me and I gasp as the cold air hits my too warm skin. Seriously, I want to duck his too gorgeous head under the water and watch with satisfaction as he sputters for air.

Yet I'm taken off guard when his gaze slides down my body. I see the heat in those blue eyes and I am strangely curious. What does he see when he looks at me? Am I a challenge because, unlike most women, I made it a point to not like him from the moment I met him?

Despite my desire to not like him, I realize I *do* like him. He's not all that horrible. Yes, he had bad habits, but who the hell doesn't? Ryder was a bad boy, and I was intrigued by the unapologetic way that he led his life, like he didn't care what anyone thought of him. *What would that be like?* I wonder. Me, who had lived an overly protected life with parents who had expected me to carry myself in a certain way, to excel at everything I set my mind to, to pull straight A's and attend a college of my mother's choosing. Don't get me wrong—I wasn't complaining about my life. I was fortunate, and there were a lot of people who wished they could trade places with me, but there were times I envied other people, like Ryder, who were free to be who they wanted to be and didn't care what anyone else thought.

His lashes are spiked, and I'm almost pissed that he has

better features than I do. Why are some people blessed with so much beauty while others...well, they have to work so much harder with what little they do have?

I remind myself that Ryder has gotten his reputation because he's used to getting his way with women, and no doubt, people in general.

As though I'm a woman possessed, I splash him in the face.

His deep laughter gives me goose bumps. It's a combination of surprise and a husky chuckle that lets me know I'm in trouble. He swims under the water, and then the entire air mattress is being rocked and a second later I'm hitting the cold water.

When I come up for air, Ryder is on my mattress with the biggest shit-eating smile I've ever seen.

"Come and get it," he says as he starts paddling toward the dock.

I wade for a few minutes, staring in disbelief as his strong arms work the mattress and he moves further and further away.

Does he seriously think I'll swim after him?

He stops about ten feet from the dock. He's now lying on his back, arms crossed under his head, looking at me with that cocky smile, daring me to follow him.

I'm so tempted to try and flip him over.

I swim toward him, glide under the water, and bypass the raft.

With my heartbeat pounding in my ears, I grab hold of the dock ladder and pull myself up.

Kenzie and Deklan are holding hands, and they both look over at me as I lay down beside Deklan.

Ryder is saying my name, and I ignore him.

"You can have your raft back," he says, his voice full of humor.

"I don't want it," I snap. Oh my God, I sound like such a bitch.

Why is it that he always manages to bring out the worst in me?

ELEVEN

R^{yder}

Curtis is staring at me.

He's been watching me the same way my mom had watched me those last weeks before she kicked me out of the house.

He knows I'm using.

Feeling like the bastard at the family picnic, I lie flat on my back on the dock and close my eyes. Trust me, I'd much rather be taking in the view of all the hot chicks at the lake parading around in their bikinis. Ange's body surprises me the most, I think. She has the tightest butt I've ever seen, and curves in all the right places.

Too bad I make her squirm. And here, for whatever reason, I had thought we'd made a connection.

Even now she's gone to the opposite side of the dock to get away from me. I hear her laughter, and I have to smile to myself. The girl is a bit contagious. I can see why Kenzie considers her such a good friend.

"You going to make practice tonight, Ryder?"

I open my eyes and squint at Brooke. I'm so not buying it. I know why she's asking me a question. I have five sets of eyes on me now. One of those sets of eyes is my best friend. Deklan sucks the lip ring into his mouth and chews on it as everyone waits for my response.

Everyone is watching me too closely. I can hardly wait to get back to land and put my sunglasses back on.

Big fucking mistake not to bring them with me out here, especially with the newly converted. Recovering addicts were the worst when it came to pointing the finger. I had to constantly bite my tongue, especially around Curtis. Everywhere I looked around the house there was some self-help book about addiction. Good for him for celebrating his sobriety and all that, but damn, I found it all so…exhausting.

It's like none of them remember the day when we all got high together, which wasn't very long ago.

Judge away, you hypocritical motherfuckers. The words were so close to coming out, but I bite the inside of my cheek to keep myself in check.

Now I felt like a kid with his hand caught in the cookie jar.

"Yeah, of course," I say. "I wouldn't miss it."

I rest my head back on the wood planking and ignore their gazes. I can't resist though—and I pop one eye open.

They're all looking away, except for Deklan.

He's the one person I don't want to disappoint. The only guy who believes in me, even more than I believe in myself.

Not that I believe in myself. I know I'm fucking weak.

I could have been two weeks clean today, but now I'm back to square one.

I'm such an idiot.

My heart continues to pound. If Deklan kicks me out of the house, then I have absolutely nowhere to go. Well, my grandparents might take me back, even after I was such an asshole to them. The small town they lived in was okay for retirees, but it was no place for me.

After a few silent minutes I hear a familiar voice.

"Hey guys."

Mr. Star Athlete is pulling his chiseled body up and onto the dock. He's alone, and his smile is directed at only one person.

And Ange is beaming as Cole takes a seat beside her. He's the biggest guy at the lake, and he knows it. I'm sure he spends at least three hours a day at the gym, and I'd bet a month's pay he takes performance-enhancing drugs.

I've heard Kenzie bitch about her brother to Deklan. I wonder how she feels about him hitting on her best friend?

I sit up on my elbows and watch little Miss Priss turn into a gushy ball of nervous energy in Cole's presence.

The conversation quickly turns to football and Cole's strenuous workouts to prepare for the upcoming season. He even has to fly to Seattle on Wednesday to take care of business, he says, chest all puffed out with self-importance.

I want to roll my eyes as he continues talking about himself.

In ten minutes he doesn't ask a single question about her. I bet if we were quizzed, I might know more about his sister's best friend than he does.

Ange asks Cole about someone named Nadia and I grin inwardly.

There's a jealous tone in her voice that's impossible not to mistake.

"She's Greg's friend," he says.

"Seems like she's *your* friend."

He laughs under his breath. "I swear to you—"

"Liar," Brooke chimes in. "That chick is all over your ass."

"Come on now...she's been dating Greg."

Cole motions toward the air mattress. "You want to go

for a swim, Ange? You don't mind if I borrow your mattress, do you, Kenz?"

"It's Curtis's mattress," Kenzie says.

Cole glances at Curtis, who replies, "Go for it, bro."

Ange's eyes widen in surprise. Why is she so stunned that he's asking her to go for a swim with him? I've heard the ten year-old boys behind us talk about how smoking hot our girls are.

Seconds later the two are floating by themselves, chatting it up and laughing.

"So how long have your brother and best friend been hitting it?" I ask, and my voice has an edge to it that shocks me.

Kenzie's brows furrow. "They're not *hitting* it."

I snort. "Could have fooled me."

"No way." She's shaking her head.

"Yeah, it is pretty obvious," Brooke says, and I'm glad that at least one of my friends has my back. "She's been staring at him all afternoon, and she was getting jealous of that leggy chick."

I'm sure it's the drugs in me, but I am seriously tempted to swim out to Ange again and get in between her and lover boy. Instead, I'm forced to watch under lowered lids. Cole is pulling the air mattress closer to him with every minute that passes.

It might have just been a trick of the light, but I swear he kissed her once. She must have been nervous because she looks our way, a guilty expression on her face.

Kenzie is watching, too. Her body language says she's not too sure about this.

"Girlfriend might be tapping big bro's ass," Brooke whispers loudly, and Kenzie frowns.

"No, I don't think so. Ange isn't interested in Cole. He's like a big brother to her…"

I have to bite my lip to refrain from saying anything more. Clearly Kenzie is in denial about the extent of her brother and her best friend's relationship.

"Interested in what?" I prompt. "In sex? Are you sure about that?"

Kenzie presses her lips together. "No way."

I can tell by Kenzie's expression that Ange is just as innocent as I thought. She was stubborn enough to put any guy in their place, but she liked Cole.

Brooke puts her hair up in a topknot. "I could tell the first time I saw the two in the same room."

"Me, too," Curtis says.

Kenzie looks at Deklan for confirmation.

Deklan shrugs. "I don't know, babe. If I had to guess, I'd say they liked each other."

Not for long, I think to myself as Ange laughs loudly at something Cole said to her.

"Cole doesn't look at Ange in that way." It's obvious to everyone that Kenzie's struggling with the information as she watches the two closely.

A^{nge}

I'm aware of the silence that follows me as I slide off the raft and walk up the beach.

The others have all made their way to shore and are watching me closely, especially Ryder. He's smiling, and yet there's something in his stare that makes me think he might be mad at me.

Yeah, I was being a bit of a bitch about the raft thing. He'd just been trying to tease me. The last thing I remember is him pushing me off my raft and taking it away from me, so why is he being a dick? All I did was splash him...and act like a baby after he'd dunked me.

Oh, wait a second, I'm talking about Ryder.

The asshole who always gets his way with everyone.

"You ready to go?" Kenzie asks me. Her tone is cool as

her gaze shifts to Cole.

"How about a quick game of Frisbee?" Cole offers.

Deklan hesitates, but Ryder steps forward. "Sure."

The guys head off to play Frisbee. Kenzie, Brooke, and I linger behind and sit beneath the shade of an oak tree.

Brooke pulls out a bottle of bright red nail polish from her purse and shakes it before she starts painting her toes.

She's unusually quiet.

The boys start a four-way game of Frisbee. Cole's already getting fancy throws in. Curtis is a little awkward and the Frisbee slips from his fingers like the disk is smothered in grease.

I glance at Brooke and she's smirking…that is, until Curtis glances her way and she flashes him a thumb's up and a reassuring grin.

Deklan makes it look easy, and Kenzie is brimming over with pride. There is a growing crowd of girls circling around, Nadia being one of them, checking out the newbies with interest.

Kenzie is well aware of the extra attention on her man, and she doesn't hesitate to throw in a "babe" when she yells out in a show of support.

I'm stunned that Ryder hasn't paid much attention to the new arrivals. Instead, his focus is on the Frisbee. He's dropped it a few times. Cole hasn't faltered once. His prowess as a quarterback is obvious to everyone around.

If Nadia claps one more time when any of the guys does a fancy move, I'm going to wring her neck.

When Curtis drops the Frisbee yet again, one of the girls nearby laughs and Brooke glances her way. "Shut the fuck up," she says loud enough for them to hear.

The girl's eyes widen, and she instantly gets up and heads for the bathroom.

Brooke stands. "I'll be right back."

Reaching up, Kenzie takes her cousin's hand. "Oh no you don't."

"What? I need to go to the bathroom." Brooke's voice is hardly convincing.

"Sit your ass down. We don't need to be restricted from this park."

Brooke slowly sits down.

Deklan is out after one more round.

Kenzie slides her arms around his neck and he lifts her up off her feet. Nadia and friends are watching every second and I smile inwardly.

Take that, bitches!

Curtis is headed our way.

And then there were two.

Save yourself, I want to yell to Ryder, but it's clear to everyone that he's determined to beat Cole.

Unfortunately, with every throw he grows more nervous and fumbles more often.

"He's using," Curtis says matter-of-factly and my stomach tightens.

Deklan flinches and frowns at Curtis. "You don't know that."

"It's pretty obvious," Brooke replies, screwing the nail polish lid on and tossing it in her bag. "I've been around Ryder long enough to know when he's straight and when he's high. He's high."

I swallowed hard, feeling uncomfortable to be part of the conversation. I didn't know Ryder before, so I couldn't comment either way. His behavior had seemed pretty much the same since I'd first met him.

Deklan runs a hand through his hair and sucks the lip ring into his mouth and chews on it.

I remember Kenzie always telling me he had the cutest habit of doing that when he was thinking or worried about something. She wasn't kidding.

"Time to have a talk with him," Curtis says, clapping Deklan on the back.

Silence follows Curtis's statement, and Deklan stares at

his best friend.

Ryder throws the Frisbee extra hard at Cole, and it hits him in the chest. Cole immediately recovers. He returns the Frisbee. It hits Ryder in the head.

"Fucking prick," Ryder says, and he's furious.

"Dude, we need to go!" Deklan practically barks the command and picks up the cooler.

I meet Kenzie's gaze and we both lift our brows.

Cole's grinning triumphantly from ear to ear, and I feel a moment of pity for Ryder. Kenzie told me about her short foray into using prescription drugs, and how for that time she felt controlled by her need to be numb and disappear.

Is that how Ryder feels? Like he wants to disappear? Instead of being grossed out, I feel empathy for him. Why does he feel like he would rather be high than experience life? I had never been high a day in my life, nor did I plan to be, but I had watched enough afterschool specials and attended enough assemblies to know I didn't want to go down that path.

We quickly pack up and Cole heads our way.

"Kenzie, are you heading out?" he asks.

"Yeah," she says. "You?"

"In a few. Tell Mom I'll be home by seven."

She nods and then looks directly at me. "You want to ride with Cole, Ange?"

My cheeks burn.

"You can...if you want to," Cole says, and I feel awkward because I can't really tell if he actually wants me to hang out or not. I just hate how Kenzie put me on the spot. She doesn't seem pissed, just confused.

"I'll ride with you," I say to Kenzie. I start walking toward the parking lot. I'm mortified and a little pissed by Cole's lack of excitement to be alone with me. I glance over my shoulder to see Nadia, standing alone, lingering by the volleyball net.

Kenzie catches up with me and puts a hand around my

elbow. "You like my brother, Ange."

It's not a question. It's more like she's stating a fact.

"I think he's hot, just like every other girl on the planet."

She adjusts the purse strap on her arm. "How come I didn't see it before now?"

"You're totally overreacting. I think Cole's cute, and we've been spending a little time getting to know each other. Christ, we're not dating." I'm getting snappy again and I have to wonder why. If I had a brother and Kenzie was fooling around with him without me knowing it, would I be pissed? Maybe...

"Am I overreacting?"

I nod. "Does it bother you to think that I'd date him?" I steady myself for her answer.

"I just don't want you to get hurt, Ange. You know how he is. He's a bit of a player. He tells me about all the hot chicks around at school."

The words cut like a knife but I won't let her know that. She's not telling me this to hurt me. She's just doing her best to protect me. She knows her brother better than anyone.

"You're my best friend and I don't want anything to ever come between us."

I release the breath I'd unconsciously been holding. "I know, Kenz. I completely understand."

I force a smile I don't feel. "Seriously, we're not dating or anything. We're just friends."

"You heading over to the boy's house?" Brooke asks, effectively ending the conversation and I'm glad. I guess I had never expected Kenzie to be unhappy about me seeing her brother.

I won't lie...it stings a little.

I look at Kenzie. "Does your mom expect us home for dinner?"

Kenzie pulls her cell from her pocket and checks the time. "I can call and put her off for a bit. Or maybe tell her we'll do our own thing. I think she actually likes it when we do that. Then she doesn't have to worry about cooking." She glances at me. "What do you want to do?"

"I'm down for going by the boy's place for a bit."

I could tell by her relieved smile that it was the answer she was hoping for.

For now, I was going to put a little bit of space between me and Cole.

TWELVE

R^{yder}

Having made myself a sandwich, I grab a bag of chips from the pantry and start down the stairs.

Music that had been playing is abruptly silenced when I take the final step into the room I call home of late.

Surrounding the couch that made out to my bed are my friends.

Fuck...

Deklan stands and he nods toward the recliner. "Have a seat, Ryder."

Brooke and Curtis are holding hands on the couch, and Kenzie and Ange are sharing an oversized chair. Both look ready to bolt.

I want to run away as well.

Appetite suddenly gone, I set my sandwich aside and take a seat.

"How long have you been using?" Brooke blurts, and Curtis puts his hand on her thigh. I'd been around them long enough to know it was his way of keeping her calm. Brooke could be a raging bitch when she wanted to be.

Although they're all staring holes into me, it is Deklan I look at. I can see in his eyes that he wants me to tell Brooke she's wrong and that I'm straight. That I've held up my part of the promise to my band and that I'd stayed drug-free.

I'm fully prepared to lie through my teeth, and basically to do anything to save my own ass, because these people are my lifeline. If it wasn't for Deklan, I'd literally be on the streets, and if it wasn't for the band, I'd have nothing to drive me to continue moving forward and facing another endless fucking day.

"I drank some cough syrup because I haven't been able to sleep for shit," I blurt out, hoping they buy it. "Too many days of no sleep was just fucking with my head too much."

Deklan runs his hands down his face and presses his palms together in a praying position, fingers resting against his lips. "You swear?"

"I swear," I say, hating myself for lying to my best friend.

"You're taking a drug test, dude," Curtis says matter-of-factly. "If it's positive, then you're out of the band." His voice has zero emotion. "Until you can get off drugs and stay off. You get clean, then you're back with open arms."

My irritation must have shown on my face because Brooke sits forward in the chair. "Ryder, we made a pact. If we break it, then what's keeping the rest of us from going off on a bender? We can't stray from the rules for one person. The rules have to apply to everyone."

My heart pounds so loud, I'm sure everyone can hear it. I don't want to be replaced again. I know that little asshole who's been coming by *Branded* keeps mentioning he plays bass. Wouldn't he just love to take over for me. "Fine, I'll take a drug test then."

Deklan clears his throat. "Gorge Days is the second

week of August and we're set to open, so everyone needs to be in top form."

I barely hear the announcement. Gorge Days is huge. Every band in the Pacific Northwest has tried to snag the gig. I *cannot* fuck this up.

Brooke and Curtis are hugging due to the news, and I'm elated…and terrified at the same time.

I have to pass this drug test.

Because if I'm out of the band, especially now that we landed Gorge Days, then I'll never forgive myself.

Deklan and I clasp hands. "Dude, you did it," I say, knowing how hard it must have been to keep it from us. And I know why he told us now. He wanted to divert the attention away from me, and probably wanted to give me motivation to keep my ass straight as well.

"Congratulations, you guys," Kenzie says. She's beaming with pride as she gives Deklan a hug.

Ange adds her congratulations as well. She won't make eye contact with me though.

All around me everyone is so happy and it's a huge cause for celebration. We've waited forever for this opportunity. I just feel regret. Major fucking regret. I need four days. Four days to piss clean and save face with my friends and bandmates.

"Gorge Days or no Gorge Days, you can't be in the band unless you're straight, Ryder. We're serious." This comes from Brooke, who can't keep the excitement off her face about the amazing news, but she is serious. I almost want to remind her about her near fatal experience with drugs not that long ago. Did she forget that I sat in a room and watched as a machine breathed for her after her overdose?

Christ, all I had done was slip a few pills.

I stand, pissed that she has sucked the joy out of this moment. "Brooke, I said I'll take a test, alright?"

Deklan steps forward. "You okay?"

"I'm fine," I say. "I'm stoked about Gorge Days. You did

it, dude. I'm proud of you."

He smiles. "We'll kill it. You just wait and see. It's just the beginning for *The Frozen*."

I glance at Ange. I expect her to be gloating after seeing me being reamed by my buddy. Instead, I swear I see a glimmer of tears in her eyes. She's uncomfortable. No wonder. She doesn't live in this world. No doubt she wishes she was back in San Diego in her high society charity ball bullshit life.

I don't want her fucking sympathy.

Miss High and Mighty, with her super-jock secret boyfriend.

She drops her gaze to the floor between us.

Kenzie doesn't say anything, but I do see sympathy there, too. If it were up to the girls, I'd probably stand a chance. Well, aside from Brooke, but she'd always been one of the guys.

I can't take it. I'm stifled in here with my best friends in the world. I want their understanding, and yet all I feel is their condemnation.

I walk past Deklan.

He grabs my arm. "Ryder."

"I'm okay. I just need to fucking breathe. All the air has been sucked out of this room." I force a smile I don't feel and he relaxes and nods.

"I'll be right back," I say, and he releases me, but not before giving me a surprisingly tight hug.

My throat tightens and I feel his heart pounding hard. Why couldn't I be the man he wanted me to be?

I'm sorry I'm such a fuck up. I want to say the words but I don't. I swallow them and pull away, go up the steps, and out onto the porch.

I take a fortifying breath of fresh air.

*If only...*I think.

If only I hadn't taken the pill at the concert.

If only I hadn't relapsed like a weak motherfucker.

I run a shaking hand through my hair and twist the strands. Like pulling my hair out from my head will help the remorse coursing through my veins.

I'm an idiot.

The screen door opens and slams.

"You okay?"

It's Ange.

I glance at her. "Yeah, just a little surprised."

She reaches up, puts a hand on my shoulder, and gives me a squeeze. "Just take the test and show them the truth."

Wow, did she honestly believe me when I said I hadn't used? Of course she did. She had probably never been around a druggie before. "I bet you wish you were on a beach in Hawaii right about now."

She shakes her head. "No way. Hawaii can't compare to spending a summer with Portland's up-and-coming rock stars."

"What must you think of us?" I say, almost to myself. I've heard the stories about her. I know she's a Catholic schoolgirl, comes from huge money, and still has her virginity intact…at least until the end of her summer break. Kenzie's brother will be sure to take care of that.

Like Kenzie, Ange is everything that is good in the world and I am as dark as night.

I want to tell her to run as fast and far as she can, back to California…away from me and what I could do to her and her innocence.

"You're great, talented, and an all-around nice guy."

I snort.

She slaps my arm. "You are."

"You're just blowing smoke up my ass."

"You'd know it if I was trying to blow smoke up your ass," she says, and I can hear the laughter in her voice.

I relax. "Just think of the stories you'll have to tell your Catholic school buddies when you get home."

"Trust me, they already know about you."

I lift my brows. "Really? Tell me everything."

"You're incorrigible, you know that?"

I smile. "Yeah, a little."

"You were a great topic of discussion. We didn't know very many bad boy rockers in the circles I ran in."

"Bad boy rockers, huh?" I lean back on my heels. "Hmmm, that has a ring to it."

"Don't let that go to your head," she says, and she's smiling.

I laugh under my breath.

"You know, I've heard of some things that might be able to help you. I mean…if you're struggling with not sleeping."

I frown.

"You mentioned taking cough syrup."

"Oh right."

She shrugs. "My mom is big into the holistic approach—you know, like yoga, acupuncture, and herbs."

"Does it work?"

"My mom says it does. Seriously, she won't take an aspirin, and she suffered with insomnia for years. Doesn't anymore though."

"I'm up for anything, but you have to remember…I don't have a lot of money."

"It's not about money. It's about you being okay."

She's serious. I see the sincerity in her eyes and I'm touched by her thoughtfulness. Of all the people in our little group, she's the last person I expect help from.

"You're alright, Ange, you know that?"

I'm surprised when she leans in and nudges my shoulder with hers. "You're just now seeing that, huh?"

Ange

I feel sorry for him.

Although Ryder had been an absolute asshole to my

best friend at one time, I can't shake the feeling of sympathy I feel toward him.

It seems like everyone is ganging up on him.

He's agreed to do a drug test, so what are they freaking out about? Obviously they were wrong about him using. I want to hug him and tell him everything will be okay.

"You want your sandwich? I can go get it for you."

"Nah, I don't have an appetite anymore."

He's putting on a brave face. I'm aware, as is everyone here, that he loves his band and that he was destroyed when he'd been kicked out of it before. For his sake, I hope he's telling the truth about not using. I want to believe him, I know that much.

He reaches up and lifts my chin with strong fingers.

My pulse leaps, and slowly his lips lower to mine and he kisses me.

I feel a strange compulsion to run.

And yet oddly, I lean into him and he deepens the kiss. My arms slide around his neck, and I'm pushing my chest against him.

His arms are around me and he squeezes me tight.

His tongue slips past my lips and I groan low in my throat as it sweeps past my teeth.

The kiss is surprisingly subtle—almost like he's waiting for a response from me.

How different this kiss is from the one I shared with Cole.

Cole, who had told me earlier today that he was looking forward to seeing me later tonight. I had felt excitement ripple through me at the declaration.

And yet now I was making out with Ryder?

Ryder! The one guy I couldn't stand. The guy who made me grit my teeth whenever I was around him. Until yesterday at least. Now I felt…differently.

Don't do it, a little voice inside my head was screaming. Ryder and I were like oil and water. We just didn't gel. He was a bad boy rocker, and I was a good girl bound for Pepperdine.

Ryder didn't have any college aspirations that I knew of, unlike Cole who would no doubt go on to take over his father's businesses.

My father would welcome Cole with open arms. His was the kind of pedigree my family had come to expect from me and my sisters when it came to our significant others.

Both of my parents would scare Ryder off with a glance, letting him know without words that he wasn't good enough for their baby daughter.

Inside I hear a gasp, and I immediately pull away.

Ryder is looking at me. Those blue eyes, dark with desire, make me think all kinds of indecent thoughts. He makes me a little weak at the knees. I'll admit it. I want to experience every single thing he can teach me. This man who has so little self-control.

The screen door opens and I don't have to look to know it's Kenzie. She clears her throat, and I jump like I've been shot.

All the text messages she'd sent me and the late night phone calls where she'd been crying about Ryder instantly come to mind.

"What are you doing?" she asks, and all I can do is swallow hard and glance at Ryder.

Big mistake.

His eyes are so heavy-lidded, and I feel sort of like I did earlier today when he looked at me when I was wearing just my swimsuit. It's like he can see straight through my clothing. That sexy look says so much.

I want him. That scares me even more than my friend's look of disbelief as her gaze shifts between me and Ryder.

The sides of Ryder's mouth lift ever so slowly. Kenzie shifts on her feet and pulls me close as he walks down the stairs and away from us.

He doesn't make it five feet before Deklan is out the

door, following him. "Ryder, where are you going?"

"For a walk." He sounds exhausted.

"I'll go with you."

Kenzie watches the two walk off into the darkness and then turns to me. "What just happened?"

I stare at the two best friends as they become spots on the horizon. "I honestly don't know. I felt bad for him. Everyone was accusing him of using and he looked so sad, so I followed him out here…and the next thing I know he was kissing me."

"Ange, you were kissing him back."

I can't very well defend myself. I did kiss him back, and damn if I hadn't loved every second of it.

I knew it, Kenzie knew it, and more importantly, Ryder knew it.

Kenzie sighs. I see the genuine concern on her face. "Ange, he will chew you up and spit you out."

"Kenzie, settle down. It was a kiss. He was just showing his appreciation."

Her brow arches. "Appreciation?"

"You hate him. I get it."

"I didn't say that."

She didn't have to. "Ryder's okay. He's—"

Brooke steps out onto the porch. "The Ryder Affect hits again."

I frown. "You both are making too big a deal out of a kiss."

"Girlfriend liked it," Brooke says with a knowing smile on her lips. "I saw how you pulled him down closer."

My cheeks grow warmer by the second.

Busted.

"Can we go?" I ask, so ready to leave before Ryder returned. I need to be alone with my scrambled thoughts.

THIRTEEN

R^{yder}

Curtis is downstairs with that little fucker Alec.

What the hell? He's already planning my replacement? I haven't even taken the piss test yet and he's bringing a fucking fourteen year-old in to replace me?

I hated to admit it, but the kid did have some serious skills. He would never have my ability to work an audience though.

Unable to stand the sound of the kid playing a difficult riff with no problem, I head for the door.

Fuck this shit.

I half expect Deklan to be on my heels. I make it a point to be quiet, so hopefully he'll just get the idea that I want to be alone.

An old lady who lives on the corner street is out watering her roses. She sees me and gives me a smile and I give her a wink.

She giggles like a girl and for the first time today I grin.

That was my problem. Maybe I was too proud, or maybe I was too fucking tired to care any longer. I was coming out of my skin, and I want to take a Xanax more than anything.

I reach for my phone, and my thumb hovers over Dac's number.

He can get me what I want, no questions asked. No one needs to know. Just something to take off the edge and make me feel more like myself and less like I'm coming undone.

How the hell do my buddies think taking me away from what I love will help with my sobriety, especially when they're shoving it down my throat?

I hit Dac's number. He doesn't pick up and I don't leave a message.

I pocket the phone and keep walking.

Five seconds later my phone buzzes with a text alert.

Dac: What's up?

Me: Stressing…

Dac: I'll be around until four.

He lives at least a mile away.

I start jogging.

All along I'm asking myself what I'm doing and coming up with a million reasons why I should stop using. One reason being a certain gorgeous girl with green eyes and reddish brown hair, who is ornery and complicated, and yet classy and kind.

Every single day I don't use is a victory, I tell myself, even as I keep running in the direction of Dac's house.

Dac is waiting for me on the porch. He's smoking a cigarette and puts it out in an overflowing ashtray that looks like it's been around for decades.

"Come on in, Ryder."

A few years older than me, Dac still lives at home. His mom was involved in a bad car wreck years ago, and that's when he started snagging her meds. Soon he was selling them at school, and then he got his own connections. It's not like he was ever obvious though. He didn't flaunt money like a lot of people in his business did. He stayed under the radar.

His mom is asleep on the couch, a soap opera blaring on the big screen television.

Dac doesn't bother to turn the volume down as we head into his room.

"So…Xanax?"

I flinch. It's pretty bad when a drug dealer knows your drug of choice.

"Yeah. Maybe an oxy or two." Oh my God, what am I thinking? I'm playing with fire.

"How many?"

"Let's go five each."

I pull out a hundred and set it on the dresser.

"And I need something that's going to help me piss clean."

Dac goes to his closet, pulls a box down, and starts rifling through it. He tosses a box onto the floor. "Drink this and you'll piss clean. Try to give yourself at least twenty-four hours though."

That shouldn't be too hard. I was scheduled to work all day tomorrow, and I don't think Deklan would push too much for the test. Curtis on the other hand was going to be a major pain in the ass.

"Does it work?"

"Goddamn right it works." He grins. "I've personally had great results with that one. It's gotten me out of a scrape or two."

I was going on the word of a dealer, but at this point it was all I had.

He puts the pills inside a small baggie and zips it closed.

"I'm getting some great smoke out of Hawaii. This shit will blow your mind."

Pot had never been my thing. "No, I don't think so."

My phone rings. I glance down. It's Deklan. "Dude, I

have to go."

Dac nods and shows me the door. "You know where to find me."

I press the button to answer, but it's too late.

The phone rings again.

I start jogging. "Hey."

"Where are you?" Deklan asks, doing his best to not sound too irritated. But I sense it all the same.

"I went for a walk."

"Hmmm." A few silent seconds pass and I clear my throat. "So what's up?"

"Uncle Steve has the keys to the apartment ready. You want to go check out our new place?"

I smile. I am so ready to get the hell out of Curtis and Terry's house. "Hell yes."

"Get your ass home, then."

The pills and pee clean kit are still in my pocket when I enter the house. Alec has left and I'm relieved. I don't need Curtis rubbing the little motherfucker in my face. It's all I can do not to tell Curtis what I think of him either, but I bite my lip to keep the peace.

Deklan comes up from the basement. "You ready?"

"Definitely."

In the truck, Deklan is watching me. "Don't worry about Alec. Curtis said he was just showing him a few techniques."

I didn't buy that for a second. "Are they really going to replace me with a sixth grader?"

Deklan frowns. "Why would you be replaced? Curtis just overreacted and thought you were high when you weren't."

He's serious. He completely trusts me and I feel like such an asshole for lying to him.

"You're not going anywhere, Ryder. I've got your back."

Those words stick with me as we walk around our new place. The apartment is better than I imagined. Sure, it smells old, like all ancient buildings do, but man, I appreciate the detail and craftsmanship in the original woodwork. There are nine-foot doors throughout and just as Deklan said, there is a bathroom and a laundry room between our bedrooms.

As lame as it sounds…I feel like I can breathe for the first time in forever.

Deklan is standing by the corner window of what will be our new living room. "Pretty amazing, huh?"

"It's nicer than I thought it would be." I join him at the window and we stare out at the surprisingly great view of the park in silence. A million different emotions are rushing through me. For a second I am half tempted to come clean. It's Deklan, after all.

When the girls arrive Deklan grins and I'm strangely relieved that they showed up before I said anything. After a quick tour, we sit on the floor, sun shining on our faces.

I could handle this, I think to myself. Just the four of us, chilling out together. I'd never been the monogamous type, but after watching Deklan and Kenzie's relationship evolve, I definitely saw the benefits.

"Wow, this is really nice," Brooke says, sounding pleasantly surprised.

Ange stands and rests her hands on the windowsill. She's leaning forward, looking out at the park. Her pert little ass looks amazing in her tight jeans. "When's move in day?" She glances over at me and my gaze shifts abruptly to her face.

I'm busted, and we both know it. She smiles and turns back to the view.

"Friday," Deklan says.

"Do you need help?" Kenzie asks, leaning against Deklan.

Deklan nods. "Of course. I'm hoping you two can help put things away. Ryder and I are both at a loss on how to organize a kitchen."

"Do you have kitchen supplies?" Kenzie asks.

Deklan winces.

"How about we all go to Ikea together?"

The suggestion had us piling into Kenzie's car and headed to Portland.

Soon I'm standing in a box store with my buddies. Ange and Kenzie are debating over some black candlestick holders while Deklan is checking out a monster size picture of a 57' Chevy that would look pretty bad-ass on our living room wall.

It was all so surreal. I had a job, our band was gaining a name for itself with a gig at Gorge Days, and now I had my own pad with my best friend.

For the first time in a long while I am looking forward to the future. I could do this…if I can just keep my shit together.

I sit on a bright red microfiber settee that I can only see sitting in a photography studio. "What do you think?" I ask, unable to keep the smile from my lips.

Deklan's lips quirk. "Uncle Steve is giving us his old furniture."

I try to recall the furniture he's referring to. "You mean the leather?"

"I think it's pleather."

I shrug. "Hey, I'd be happy with lawn furniture."

"Me, too. It's gonna be amazing, bro. You wait and see."

A^{nge}

I'm eating a bagel with cream cheese in the kitchen when Cole walks out of the bathroom with steam following in his wake.

"Good morning, ladies."

The bagel gets caught in my throat. He's wearing a wife beater and pajama pants, and I can smell his body spray from here.

"You okay?" Kenzie asks.

I nod, ignoring the heat that is racing up my neck to my cheeks.

Melissa is beaming. "Good morning, sweetie. I hope I didn't wake you up this morning."

Kenzie glances at me and rolls her eyes. Melissa's favoritism toward her oldest is borderline nauseating.

"I'm used to waking up early for practice anyway." He flashes her a winning smile. "I just hope one day you'll have a three bedroom apartment so at least I'll have my own room when I visit."

"From your lips to God's ears," she says, ruffling her hand through his wet, slicked back hair.

She pours herself a cup of coffee and returns to her room.

"You want to grab a shower next?" Kenzie asks.

I shake my head. "No, you go ahead." I watch as she leaves the kitchen and heads towards the bathroom.

Cole grabs an apple out of the crystal bowl on the kitchen counter and takes a bite. We are sitting side by side, and his hand is moving up and down my thigh. It's small stuff, but I know he wants more.

He got home really late last night and I had wondered who he'd been out with. I know it wasn't my place to ask him, and yet my curiosity was getting the best of me. I imagined the leggy Nadia from the lake.

"So what are you up to today?" he asks, tossing the partially eaten apple into the trashcan.

"We're heading to the farmer's market and then the guys have a concert tonight."

Cole nods. "Sounds like fun. I don't have anything going. Mind if I tag along?"

It takes me a second to realize he was being serious. I sincerely doubt that Kenzie would want him to come hang out with us. They manage to be polite around each other, but it was pretty obvious to those who knew them best that the relationship is strained.

"I'll ask Kenzie and make sure it's okay. I don't know how it works with the band passes, you know."

"Don't you want me there?"

His eyes hold mine for a few seconds, and I realize that there's a part of me that doesn't want him there. "Of course I do."

Leaning in, he kisses me softly. He pulls back the slightest bit and stares into my eyes. "I want you so much."

My stomach tightens into a knot.

The doorbell rings.

I jump a foot.

He laughs under his breath and stands to answer the door.

A squeal sounds a second before a girl throws herself into Cole's arms.

"Payton, what are you doing here?" Cole sounds alarmed.

Payton must have caught on to Cole's reaction, because the sweet smile on her face turns into a frown. "I came to see you!"

He puts her at arm's length. "Payton, I'm headed home this weekend."

Her eyes widen. "You're mad I'm here, aren't you?"

"No, of course not. I just wasn't expecting you." He forces a smile. "A call would have been nice."

"I'm sorry—" Seeing me, her eyes go even wider and she looks back at Cole with a questioning look on her face.

"This is—"

"Hi, I'm Ange," I say, extending my hand. "I'm Kenzie's best friend from San Diego."

She immediately relaxes and takes my hand. "It's lovely to meet you."

Payton is adorable. Standing just over five feet tall, with long brown hair with big curls, she stares at me with her beautiful brown eyes.

We even dress a similar way. She had on a sundress with a cute little sweater over the top. "Is that the new Bende' collection?" I ask, and she grins, showing deep adorable dimples.

"Yes, the new fall line."

"Gorgeous," I say, pouring myself a cup of coffee. I hate coffee, but I need to keep myself busy.

I listen as the two make small talk.

Cole glances at me, and I force a smile. "I have to get going. Kenzie and I are heading out to a concert tonight with the boys."

If possible, Payton's smile broadens as she slips her hand into Cole's. "It was so nice meeting you."

Cole, on the other hand, doesn't look very happy at all.

Kenzie walks out of the bathroom. "We have twenty minutes." She stops short when she sees Payton. "Hey," she says, the word sounding like a question.

"You must be Kenzie." Payton is beaming. "I recognize you from the pictures."

They make quick work of the introductions. Payton talks non-stop, and all Kenzie has to do is nod and answer in one syllable responses.

When Deklan and Ryder arrive, Payton looks a little alarmed. I am amused, because for the first time, I don't see the overwhelming sense of excitement that comes over women when they see the two. Or maybe I had misread the situation, because her gaze keeps shifting between the two men. Finally, she gasps. "Oh my God, you're *The Frozen*."

"You know them?" I ask, surprised that someone from out of town recognizes them.

"You guys played at the Puyallup County Fair a couple of summers ago. I live in Orting."

"Nice little town," Deklan responds and shakes her hand.

"It's nice meeting you both. Just wait until I tell my friends that I met you. They are going to be so jealous."

Payton looks at Cole. "How could you have failed to tell me that your sister is dating the drummer of *The Frozen*?"

"He's also the founding member of the band," Ryder is quick to add.

Deklan shifts on his feet, and I find it sweet that he's so humble.

Cole looks irritated that she's so excited about meeting the band.

"You guys want to come to the concert tonight?" Ryder asks, and I know it's all Kenzie can do not to kick him in the nuts and drop him to his knees.

***

We walk through Farmer's Market but I see little. I'm still confused by what had just happened. Cole had been kissing me two seconds before his girlfriend, who I hadn't heard of, nor had his family heard of, had showed up at the door. And now they were going to the concert with us tonight.

Kenzie is doing her best to keep me in good spirits… but I'm struggling.

I'm pissed. How could Cole have been so deceitful? I'd asked him about dating at college and he said he didn't have time with football.

Freaking liar.

I pull out of it and smile when Deklan buys Kenzie a huge bouquet of flowers. Not to be outdone, Ryder buys me a bouquet of daisies.

When we arrive back at Kenzie's apartment, we put our bouquets in vases. I'm almost disappointed Cole isn't here to see me walk through the door with flowers from Ryder.

He had left a message on the counter telling Kenzie to give him a call so we could drive over to the concert together.

Kenzie calls him and he's up the road at a restaurant. He tells us to stay put and he'll be right here.

I so wish he'd reconsider and just stay home with his girlfriend.

No such luck. Payton is glowing with happiness as they walk in the apartment, hand in hand. She's changed into a sleek, sexy black dress. It's very similar to a dress I own, and I'm reminded yet again of how alike we are.

I change into skinny jeans, and borrow one of Kenzie's shirt that shows off the better part of my back. I finish off the outfit with sexy boots.

My mom would definitely not approve of the outfit.

Kenzie's does my makeup and it's difficult for me to look in the mirror. I look different.

Ryder grins when he sees me. "You look great, Ange," he says, and gives a wink.

"Thanks," I reply, glancing at Cole.

He barely looks at me.

Payton gushes about how good we look.

"Payton, we might have to take some equipment in the car with us, so you should probably drive just in case," Deklan suggests, and I'm so relieved.

The four of us pile into the car. Ryder is driving, and he keeps watching me in the rearview mirror.

I quickly look away.

"You okay?" Kenzie asks me for like the eightieth time in as many seconds.

"Of course." I force a smile. "Why wouldn't I be?"

I half expect to see a sly grin on Ryder's face, but there isn't one. As though sensing my mood, he cranks the music a little louder and I sit back and stare out the window.

How ironic when I had felt so close to the finish line that suddenly it's like the rug is ripped out from underneath me. Cole and I had been getting closer. We were comfortable, friendly, and yes, even a bit overly flirtatious…and it had been fun while it had lasted.

"We don't even know if they're dating," Kenzie says matter-of-factly.

"She came by herself, Kenz. A girl doesn't do that unless they're dating a guy."

"You're prettier."

"Drop it," I whisper and she nods, but she's pissed at her brother. I am, too.

"I wished he would have just stayed home. I mean, it's not like he's ever gone out of his way to invite us to his events."

"We did go to all the bonfires at his football games."

"Yeah, but that's different. Everyone went to those games. It was a family outing. But this, this is my life and the last thing I need is him coming home and talking shit about my boyfriend and his band," she whispers.

I completely understand her concern. I would feel the same way, especially if my relationship with my brother was as strained as her relationship with Cole.

When we arrive at the venue, I feel calmer.

Ryder opens the car door for me and even grabs my hand to help me out.

Cole and Payton are approaching, and Ryder doesn't bother to drop my hand. He even tucks it into his elbow and we start walking. Deklan and Kenzie are five steps ahead of us, hands entwined. He leans down and kisses her cheek and I smile.

Ryder does the same to me and I nearly trip over my feet.

Normally I would tell him to knock it off already, and yet I'm strangely relieved and endeared by his effort to make me feel better. "You look sexy." His voice has a soft, sultry quality to it that I feel all the way to my bones.

"Thanks."

I glance over my shoulder. Payton and Cole are holding hands as they walk our way, but Cole's staring at my ass.

I step closer to Ryder, and he squeezes my hand in his. "You'll have a great night," he says. "Just wait and see."

FOURTEEN

A^{nge}

We are immediately ushered into the theater while the guys go in search of Brooke and Curtis. For the first time, we had seats, and I was grateful to not be watching from side stage.

I make sure to sit furthest away from Cole. It was just… awkward.

"So…how long have you been going out with my brother?" Kenzie asks the second Cole got up to get some munchies.

"We've been seeing each other exclusively for about five months now."

"That's great," Kenzie says, fake smile in place.

"My little sister misses him so much that she nearly fought me to come."

"Does she go to UW as well?"

"No, she's a sophomore in high school, but because my family lives so close, we visit a lot on weekends…that is, when Cole isn't busy with the team." Payton glances at Kenzie. "I am so excited to finally meet your mom. I wanted to before, but Cole said it just wasn't the right time. She's an amazing woman. I respect her so much."

"She's great," I agree, and Kenzie quickly looks away.

Payton looks concerned as her gaze shifts between us. She was so eager to please.

The lights are dimmed and the crowd screams as *The Frozen* steps out onto the stage.

From the corner of my eye I notice Cole making his way to his seat, hands full of drinks and candy.

I am used to the preliminaries, to Brooke's introduction of the band…and each members' bio. Ryder always got the most screams, and of course, he ate it up, flashing a wolfish smile while running his fingers along the bass strings.

"Look who's here," Kenzie says, motioning toward our right.

The slutty brunette Ryder had been with during his last concert is here with the same group of friends. Tonight she's wearing a low-cut shirt and barely there shorts. She's screaming out Ryder's name. I'm almost embarrassed for her, especially when he isn't making an effort to look her way.

I watch Payton and Cole from the corner of my eye. They are still holding hands, and I notice how she looks up at Cole often with a smile on her face.

As much as I want to not like her, I can't help it. I understood her. I knew her. Actually, I was her. We were both good girls who liked the high-school quarterback.

I sit back in my seat and let the music wash over me. During the remainder of the song, I watch the band, not paying any attention to anyone in particular. That is, until I feel Ryder's gaze on me.

Ryder walks to the front of the stage about five feet

from me and plays the bass like a man possessed. He stares at me the entire time. His hips are thrust forward, and the way he plays is so sexy.

The crowd is clapping in appreciation and staring at me.

I feel my cheeks burn.

I knew Ryder well enough to realize what he was doing. He never cared for Cole from the time they'd met.

Ryder motions me up to the stage.

My eyes widen and I shake my head.

He nods and continues to crook his finger.

Shit.

Kenzie laughs and nudges me toward him.

With hundreds of *The Frozen* fans watching me, I decide it is in my best interest to get off my butt and do as Ryder asks or risk being booed out of the venue.

I take a few steps and look up at him with an expression that I hope screams, *Don't you dare embarrass me!*

He shifts the guitar so that it swings around to his back and lifts me up on the stage.

"What are you doing?" I ask, and he smiles in a way that makes the hair on my arms stand on end.

The crowd roars their approval.

His arm slides around my side. His hand splays on my lower back and he pulls me close. His other hand cups my face as he leans in and kisses me. I'm not sure what I expected, but the soft, firm kiss wasn't it.

It's…nice.

He kisses me again, like he is testing me, and then his tongue licks the seam of my mouth and I can't remember anything after.

Every inch of my body is bathed in warmth, and there's an incessant humming in my ears.

Seconds, or maybe even minutes later, Ryder is pulling back and looking down at me with a satisfied expression on his face.

I'm aware of many things at once—like how had my arms gotten around his neck, and how had I possibly forgotten that I was in an auditorium with hundreds of people watching me make-out with a gorgeous rocker?

I abruptly step back, and it's a good thing Ryder had a hold of me, because I would have fallen off the stage.

He pulls me back to safety and then walks me to side stage.

I want to run for the closest exit.

Instead, I do my own little walk of shame…back to my seat, and back to my best friend who was giving me a, "I can't believe you just did that" grin.

Her brother doesn't look nearly as pleased. His girlfriend does though. Payton flashes me a grin and thumb's up.

What had Brooke called it—The Ryder Affect? She wasn't kidding, was she? I had just lost all track of time up there, and I can still feel the heat of that kiss in every inch of my body.

Talk about exactly what a kiss should be.

I press my lips together and try to focus on the song. My gaze keeps straying to Ryder, and each time he's looking right at me.

Maybe I hadn't exactly been fair to him since the time we met. I'd judged him. *Rightfully so*, I thought, because he'd screwed over Kenzie, yet I knew the reason he had singled me out tonight was to make me feel better. To basically give Cole a big ol' fuck you, and I found that endearing in its own way.

Feeling slutty girl staring at me, I dare to look her way.

Sure enough, I receive the look of death from Ryder's one-time fling.

I quickly glance away, and keep my gaze focused on Brooke. It's tough, especially when Ryder's staring at me.

After the encore, the four of us make our way to the backstage room where the band is lounging.

Deklan stands as soon as he sees Kenzie, and she goes into his arms.

"Have a seat," Brooke says, motioning toward a couch that is lined in plastic.

"Go ahead," I say to Cole and Payton, trying not to think of what had happened on that plastic covered couch.

"I'll be right back," Ryder says.

Payton sits and seems positively giddy as she looks around.

I know what she's thinking. I had felt the same excitement during my first concert. I was elated to be a part of it, having to practically pinch myself when I'd been side stage.

It had been a world that was so far removed from my own, and I knew I'd never forget this summer for as long as I lived.

"So what did you think of the concert?" Brooke asks.

"Amazing. Thank you so much for inviting us," Payton says, looking at Deklan. "I won't stop talking about it for weeks."

Brooke glances at her cousin. "And you, Cole...what did you think?"

"Yeah, it was good." His voice sounds far from convincing.

"I'll take good," she says with a laugh.

"You guys ready to get out of here?" Deklan asks, already heading for the door. "We have a big move tomorrow, so we need some rest."

"What about our equipment?" Curtis asks.

"Should be ready for us to load up."

Cole chips in and helps the guys load the equipment in the vehicles while Payton stands back with me, Kenzie, and Brooke.

"So...are you and my cousin pretty serious?" Brooke asks Payton point blank.

Payton seems a bit hesitant to answer. "Yes, we're pretty

serious. I mean, we agreed to be exclusive."

That was the second time the word had come up.

"Exclusive, huh?" Brooke gives her a little nudge on the shoulder. "Good for you."

"You make a good couple," I say, and Brooke gives me an odd look.

Payton brightens. "Thank you. You know, my family just adores Cole."

"Wow, that does sound serious." Brooke glances at me, and lifts a brow.

"Let's go, ladies!" Curtis motions for us to follow, and I'm relieved for the interruption.

I immediately notice that Ryder is still M.I.A., and I wonder if he's with slutty girl. Whatever…if that's the kind of girl he wants. I mean, what kind of girl has sex in the closet with a guy within minutes of meeting him?

I chew on my thumbnail as I wait for Ryder to appear.

"You're so quiet," Kenzie says, and I give her a reassuring smile.

"I'm just a little tired, that's all."

"Yeah, I'm ready for bed, too."

"You're not coming by?" Deklan doesn't hide his disappointment.

"Maybe we'll spend the night tomorrow," Kenzie says, and I hit her on the shoulder.

"A sleepover." Ryder appears from behind me. He sounds and looks way too smug.

"Yeah, we'll celebrate the first night at your new place with a slumber party." Kenzie is all excited, but my stomach is already in knots at the thought.

Deklan reaches back and grabs Kenzie's hand. "Sounds good, babe."

I catch Ryder's gaze in the rearview mirror. The kiss we'd shared on stage had been heated. So heated I had lost track of time. What would happen if we spent the night together?

I glance at Deklan and Kenzie's entwined hands. Once again, I wonder if I will ever have what they have. One day, I promise myself. One day…

FIFTEEN

A^{nge}

I step out of the shower and let out a gasp.

Cole is standing with his back to the sink, arms crossed over his chest, a shit-eating grin on his face. His gaze shifts over my body slowly. Thank God I had dried off in the shower and hadn't unwittingly flashed him. I tuck the edges of the towel into place.

"Hey."

I look down to make sure all my body parts are securely covered. "What are you doing?"

"So what was that?" His tone is clipped and curt.

I clear my throat. "What do you mean?"

"The little show at the concert."

"Ryder kissed me."

"Yeah, I got that."

Was he seriously mad about Ryder pulling me on

stage when he was with his girlfriend, who he had failed to mention since I arrived in Vancouver? "It was a surprise. I didn't know Ryder was going to do that."

He snorted. Obviously he didn't believe me. "You didn't seem to mind it."

I drop my gaze to the floor. "It wasn't horrible." My eyes widen in surprise. Oh my God, what had I been thinking? Why would I say that?

"Uh, yeah, apparently not. You were all over him. I'm surprised you were able to stand after that kiss."

I'm not sure what he wants from me.

"How is it that you failed to tell me about your girlfriend?"

He swallows hard. "Payton and I are just dating."

"You said you had no time to date because football kept you so busy."

Apparently I've rendered him speechless. He shifts on his feet.

"She says you're exclusive and have been for months."

He runs a hand through his hair, the motion making the muscle in his arm flex. I'm trying to forget the way I've felt about him for so many years. Cole had been the object of my affection forever. I had compared every other man to him, and every other man had come up lacking.

And yet lately, just the way he talks shit about Kenzie and her friends and his better-than-everyone-else attitude makes me irritated. Payton's arrival was the icing on the cake.

"Sure, she's a nice girl…but so are you." He steps closer and I take a step back, nearly ending up on my ass if I hadn't caught myself.

"You've been kind of clumsy of late," he says, his gaze shifting to my cleavage. "Come lie down with me? The couch is comfortable," he says with his charming smile.

"Isn't your girlfriend coming over in the morning?"

"Payton will be over tomorrow afternoon. She's staying

with her aunt in Longview and wants to spend the morning with her."

"You'd better get to bed then."

I was so glad I'd be gone tomorrow afternoon…and tomorrow night. I need time away from Cole to understand where my thoughts are. I feel so confused.

He sighs loudly. "I'm not tired."

"I'm exhausted and I have a busy day tomorrow, so I need to get some rest."

"Please…just lie down with me for a little bit."

It's so unlike Cole to say please. I don't know what it was…maybe those gorgeous eyes of his, or maybe I just needed to get him out of the bathroom so I could get dressed and pull my thoughts together. He was my best friend's brother, so I needed to at least stay on friendly terms with him.

I enter the living room ten minutes later and hesitantly lay down beside him on the hide-a-bed.

"No touching," I say, and he nods but cozies up to me.

We watch a movie and as the minutes tick away I start to relax, not minding as the front of his thighs touch the backs of mine. Soon his hand slides across my waist and he snuggles tighter to me.

"I said no touching."

He smiles.

Just the smell of him is overwhelming. Pure, unadulterated male.

His thumb brushes back and forth over my ribcage.

I swallow hard.

I glance up at him, and before I can blink, he's kissing me.

I don't push him away. I know I should. Everything within me tells me to. This isn't right. He has a girlfriend. A nice girlfriend, and yet my willpower dissipates as he moans softly.

Oddly, I can't help but compare the kiss to the one I

shared with Ryder. Ryder's lips were so soft, and yet firm... and I'd enjoyed how tentative he was about the kiss— as though he was waiting for me to be the one to deepen the kiss or end it. This kiss isn't like that. No, Cole is the aggressor, and as his tongue sweeps into my mouth it's like he's demanding an answer. For an instant I'm inclined to pull away.

Again, my curiosity wins out.

His technique is less controlled than Ryder's. Ryder knows exactly what he's doing. His sexuality is effortless. I've heard from other girls at my school that some guys don't like to kiss at all. Sure, they'll give you a peck but they don't full on make-out...not even while having sex. They just don't like it, I guess.

I remember Kenzie telling me about her first night with Ryder. How he'd intently stared into her eyes, and how into her he'd been, and how it felt like no one else existed.

Cole's hand moves up my ribcage to my breast and I stiffen.

He deepens the kiss even more.

I don't have time to think any longer.

His fingers dip beneath the edge of my bra, and then his hand is palming my breast.

The breath freezes in my lungs.

Until he plucks at my nipple.

His lips leave mine, and he's kissing my neck, and then the curve of my breast.

My breasts are exposed as he pulls my bra straps down and unhooks my bra. He's kissing my breast, his mouth hovering over a nipple. His tongue lightly touches the sensitive bud.

Okay, this feels amazing. It does...

Despite the overwhelming sensations exploding inside my body, warning signs are going off in my head, and yet I can't find the words to say no.

Because I really don't want to say no.

I want more.

And he gives me exactly what I'm asking for.

His hand moves down my stomach, and he reaches for my panties. He palms my sex.

My breath lodges in my throat.

And then his hand is inside the silk of my panties, and he's sliding the tip of his finger along my clit.

He makes little circles around the tiny bundle of nerves.

I lift my hips, enjoying what he's doing and wanting more.

As something builds within me, more intense with each stroke of his finger, I groan low in my throat.

He releases a little laugh and then he rolls and he's on me. An elbow is on either side of me, and he's staring down at me intensely. I sense a question in those eyes.

I feel his hard cock against me.

His hips flex and he moans low in his throat and kisses me.

He begins to move, and I'm confused. Our clothes are on.

Any second I expect him to take down our pants but he doesn't. He keeps moving and I get caught up in the moment as well. This feels good, the friction just enough that I feel my body moving toward a pinnacle that I know will be amazing.

I can't help it. I lift my hips toward him, over and over again, and he's thrusting against me. The kiss intensifies.

Cole thrusts faster, and he's no longer kissing me. "Oh God," he groans into my hair, a second before I feel a warm wetness against my stomach and realize with a start what's happened.

He actually came.

I'm not sure what stuns me more—the fact that he had fucked me with my clothes on, or that he had gotten off and left me wanting.

He rolls off me, a hand over his forehead.

There is a wet stain on his pajama pants, and on mine

as well.

He had obviously found his release. I couldn't say the same for myself. I feel like a string ready to snap. As the minutes tick by, the intense sensations that had built in my groin now starts to ebb…and I have my first experience at sexual frustration.

I hear a door open and I freeze. Cole draws the sheet up and over us. Thank goodness there is space between us. I'm resting on my elbow, hoping I look casual and at ease, when Melissa walks into the kitchen.

I am horrified at the prospect that she might have heard us.

She has her robe on and she opens the fridge and grabs a pint of ice cream. When she glances over at us, she looks surprised to see me in bed with her son.

"Oops…busted," she says, and I hope she's talking about the ice cream in her hand, and not about catching us in bed together.

"Midnight munchies?" Cole says.

I wish my pajama pants weren't wet and my bra wasn't unhooked, or I'd just get up and walk to Kenzie's room.

"Unfortunately, yes. It's become a habit of mine, and my waistline is suffering because of it."

"You look great, Mom," Cole says.

"You're sweet for saying so, even though I know it's a lie." She gives me a wink. "Well, you kids get to bed soon."

"We will," Cole and I say in unison.

The second I hear her door close I get up and hook my bra.

Cole's gaze drifts to my pajama pants. I can't tell if he's embarrassed or not. Maybe dry humping is something he does regularly. At least I'm still a virgin.

"Good night," I say.

He reaches out and grabs me by the wrist. "Wait a second. No goodnight kiss?"

I lean down and he kisses me softly. "Sweet dreams," he

whispers against my lips.

I linger for a second, and I'm not sure what I'm waiting for. He releases me and I have no choice but to return to Kenzie's room.

Thank God she's sleeping. I change my underwear and pants and slide into bed beside my best friend.

Before I know it I'm crying, and I can't put my finger on why I'm so upset. Maybe it's the disappointment of having such a high expectation and the reality was just such a let down. Would I actually feel better right now if we'd removed our pajamas and had sex? Or would I feel even worse than I do right now?

I'm pretty sure I'd feel worse if we'd actually had sex.

I thought of the kiss with Ryder earlier that night. I hadn't felt even a smidgen of guilt. I hadn't. In fact, I had appreciated him making me feel desired.

I was never sure if Cole was just afraid to take our friendship out of the friend zone, or if he was worried about what Kenzie and her mom would say. Now I knew he had a girlfriend, and from all accounts, they were really serious.

But you didn't do anything wrong. At least that's what I try to convince myself, even as I continue to cry and fall into a fitful sleep.

Ryder

Lying on my bed, I stare at the ceiling.

My entire body is shaking. I want a fucking pill so bad I can't stand it.

Deklan had crashed a few minutes ago and I hear him moving around in his room. I wait until I hear the creak of his bed before I get up and go toward the fridge, and most notably, the freezer, where there is a fifth stashed.

Tequila definitely isn't my drink of choice, but beggars can't be choosers. I wince when the bottle makes a clinking sound as I remove it.

I'm hiding behind the door of the refrigerator, so even if Deklan walks out, I can hide what I'm doing. I unscrew the cap and take a long swig.

The liquor burns its way down my throat and I welcome it.

I have pills I can take, but I can't do it. Not unless I know I don't have to take the piss test.

Honestly, I hope the band has forgotten about the drug testing. Tonight I played better than I had in weeks. Deklan was surprised that I'd pulled Ange on stage, and yet he told me understood why I had done it, and he had even managed a smile as though to say he would have done the same thing if he'd been in the same position.

I take another long drink before I replace the cap and set it back inside the freezer.

Sliding under the sheets of my uncomfortable bed, I wonder what is happening over at Kenzie's house. Payton had said she was staying the night with a family member who lived thirty miles north of Vancouver, which meant Cole and Ange were probably keeping each other comfortable.

I grit my teeth just thinking about Cole and Ange.

He would tell her everything she wanted to hear. *No, baby, I'm not dating Payton. She's just a friend. Don't worry about it.*

I know all the lines, all the moves, all the excuses. I've made them. Hell, I'd been busted screwing Kenzie's friend red-handed and I'd still denied it.

Girls believed what they wanted to believe. They would turn on their friend before they would turn on their man, even if that friend was the one who had fooled around with their man.

I think of Ange tonight as she watched me on stage. When I'd pulled her up there, she'd wanted to knock me out. I could see it in her eyes, and yet she'd surprised me in all the right ways when she'd kissed me back and so willingly.

Amber, the brunette from the janitor's closet, had pulled me aside afterward. "You never called me," she had said, managing a pout.

"I've been so busy," had been my lame excuse as I had kept one eye on the backstage door, just waiting for Ange to walk out.

"Can I come home with you?" Her eyes were so desperate, and I honestly felt bad for her. She had a sorry life ahead of her if she continued to spend her nights attending concerts and having meaningless sex with men who would never treat her the way she yearned to be treated. "No, not tonight." It hurt to say those words. She looked hurt. I had used her and we both knew it.

But Ange.

She was different.

She was a good girl with an attitude. Someone who was destined to do amazing things in her life and have opportunities that most people could only wish for.

I'm amazed she's managed to hang with us and even enjoy herself. If her parents could see her now, they would probably be horrified, I think with a smile, actually laughing when I remember her splashing me in the face at the lake. Even she'd been surprised by her reaction.

Little did she realize I had gotten under her skin.

She was just one more reason for me to stay straight.

Tomorrow was another day. Tomorrow would be easier, I tell myself as I turn off the bedside light and hope for sleep to come.

SIXTEEN

A^{nge}

By five o'clock the following afternoon we had Deklan and Ryder's new apartment pretty much put together. The guys had spent their time doing all the heavy lifting, while Kenzie, Brooke, and I unloaded boxes, putting the kitchen, bathrooms, and living room together.

I had noticed that Deklan had given Kenzie carte blanche on picking out everything for the kitchen, but when it came to art—he had a specific taste and he had chosen pictures. The gothic style mirror in the entryway had been Ryder's choice.

"Deklan's credit card has to be hurting right about now," Brooke says, and neither one of us argues with her. He had already dropped a pretty penny at a few stores in Portland and Vancouver.

"He's excited though," Kenzie adds. "He's never had his

own place."

Brooke snorts. "Yeah, well, it's not like he's living alone."

"Yeah, but living with Ryder is different," Kenzie says, and I can see she's getting defensive of her man and his choice to have his best friend move in with him.

"No, I get it." Brooke stifles a yawn and glances at the clock on the stove. "Anyone else starving?"

"Yeah. Deklan mentioned a pizza place a few blocks over off of Reserve street," Kenzie says, handing Brooke a few twenty dollar bills. "You want to head over and order for us? The guys like—"

"Dude, I know what kind of pizza they like," Brooke says, pocketing the money. "I can't tell you the amount of pizza we've eaten during practice jams."

"True," Kenzie says, and hoists herself up on the counter.

"I'll call you when it's close to being ready." The door closes behind Brooke.

Silence follows her departure. I feel Kenzie's stare on me. "You've been so quiet today. What's wrong?"

I shake my head. "Nothing." I continue unloading glasses from the dishwasher and place them into the cupboard.

"Mom said that you were watching TV with Cole last night. Did something happen between you two?"

"No," I snap, and immediately wish I'd kept my mouth shut. She knew me too well. No matter how much I tried to fake it and be happy, it just never seemed to work. Kenzie could always sense when something was wrong.

And she was right. All day I'd been stressing about what had happened last night with Cole. I couldn't believe, especially after meeting Cole's girlfriend, that I had allowed things to go so far.

We could have so easily had sex, and I would have woken up without my virginity...and he would probably drop me like a hot rock.

"I know it was tough with Payton showing up last night, and then them going to the concert with us. Nothing like having your nose shoved in it."

"Payton is nice," I say, a little too quickly.

Kenzie frowns. "That's the second time I've heard you say it."

"I mean it. She *is* nice, and she and Cole make a good couple. It was just a silly schoolgirl crush anyway. I live in California, and he lives in Washington. It's not like it would ever go anywhere."

"One day Cole will move back to San Diego though. I'm sure Dad expects him to run his businesses when he retires." She squeezes my hand. "If you like him, then don't give up."

I didn't understand why I felt this way. Ironically, Cole had behaved a lot in the way I had hoped. He'd paid attention to me, and actually moved really fast and let me know that he liked me. I had always hoped and fantasized that we'd be the ultimate couple. That I would see him when he came to San Diego to see his dad, and I could fly up to Seattle once every couple of months and visit him.

It had all seemed so easy then.

Now it seemed completely unrealistic.

And of course, I hadn't included a Payton, or any other girl, in the picture. Now it was complicated, and I didn't see the happily ever after I had originally envisioned.

Heavy footsteps come up the staircase and we both go quiet.

Deklan opens the door and pops his head in. "Hey, we have the couch. Want to help clear the way here?"

"Sure," Kenzie and I say in unison, moving aside the mostly empty boxes.

"We're going to have to turn and lift," Curtis says, cussing under his breath. "Jesus, we might have to cut this fucker in two in order to make it fit."

I hear Ryder laugh, and the sound makes me smile.

"Dude, we're going to have to unscrew the feet." Ryder is already unscrewing one of them, while Deklan starts on the other.

I glance at Ryder. Dressed in a white sleeveless t-shirt and ratted out jeans, he is the epitome of sexy.

Last night the way he'd pulled me on stage and kissed me in front of everyone—it's like the world had stopped for a short space of time. He hadn't made it weird afterward, even if I was a bit embarrassed by my reaction.

I tried not to think about Cole. Maybe a part of me just felt…dirty. I did one thing I told myself I would never do… and that was to go after a taken man. I knew, by way of my best friend at least, how it felt to be on the receiving end of an unfaithful boyfriend. I swore I would never be that kind of girl.

I had been exactly that kind of girl last night. What horrified me more than anything was how easily I could have gone to the next level. I'd been so caught up in the moment and lost all sense of control that I had forgotten that I actually was with someone who had made a commitment to another person.

Payton's declaration that she and Cole were exclusive haunts me today.

Curtis's phone rings.

"We'll be right there," he says. "Brooke said the pizza will be ready in five. Let's get over there."

We walk to the small pizza shop. I'm a few steps behind the group and watch as Ryder lights a cigarette. He rests his head back on his shoulders and releases a long, steady stream of smoke into the air.

He glances back at me, stops and waits for me to catch up.

"Are you okay?" he asks.

Oh my God, was I that obvious? I nod. "Yeah, definitely. Just a little tired."

"Okay, I thought maybe I said something…"

"No."

Once again, I feel close to tears. I had just had my period, so I had no excuse as far as blaming my emotional status on PMS. Nope, definitely just men problems in general. If I had been home, I would feign a sick day, curl up in bed, and sleep the day away. I couldn't very well do that here, especially when the guy who was causing me so much mental anguish was sleeping twenty feet away in the next room.

Ryder slides his arm around my shoulders and brings me in for a hug.

I push him gently. "I hate the smell of smoke."

He drops the cigarette and crushes it beneath his shoe.

"Now you're going to litter."

"Wow, you're busting my balls today." He stops, picks up the destroyed cigarette, and tosses it in the garbage bin.

The others have walked ahead of us. He puts a hand on either one of my shoulders and squeezes. "I'm here for you if you need me." My stomach tightens at the contact.

I know Ryder is going through his own stuff, what with dealing with his recovery and facing roommates who thought he had relapsed. It was nice for him to think of me. I suddenly felt extremely selfish.

"Come on, you two!" It's Curtis, and he's keeping the restaurant door open for us.

"Promise me you'll let me know if you need something."

"I promise."

Brooke has saved us a booth in the packed restaurant. I slide in beside Kenzie and Deklan, and Ryder sits with Curtis and Brooke. I sit directly across from Ryder.

He takes a sip of pop and I stare as he is talking to Deklan about things that they still need to pick up at the old house.

I take in everything about him. The way his lower lip is pretty full, how long his eyelashes are, how blue his eyes could get, how high those cheekbones are. My gaze slides to the hands around the glass. They're strong, the fingers long, and I can only imagine what those hands can do. I remember him playing the bass, how those fingers had danced over the strings with such skill.

"Do I even want to know what you're thinking?"

I glance up and those blue eyes are staring straight at me. The sides of his mouth are lifted and his brows are furrowed.

"Probably not," I say. My voice has a touch of flirt to it, and I quickly reach for my pop and proceed to knock it over...right in Ryder's lap.

I freeze. I'm horrified as everyone in the restaurant turns to look our way.

"Oh my God, Ryder. I'm so sorry."

He stands up slowly. His belly and crotch are soaked.

Oddly I think of last night and the little event with Cole, and I want to cry all over again.

Brooke hands him the silver napkin holder and he pulls a couple out and does his best to soak up the excess.

A woman in her early twenties walks over and gives Ryder a towel. She cleans up the mess and gets me another pop.

I continue to apologize profusely. She shrugs it off, and I'm grateful. I just wish everyone would quit looking.

"I'm going to change," Ryder says, heading for the door. "I'll be right back."

I'll go with you. I want to say the words but they stick in my throat, and instead I watch his retreating back as he leaves.

The table falls silent until Brooke makes a comment about the upcoming concert. I'm grateful no one made me feel like more of an asshole than I already do.

I only partially listen to the conversation around me. I'm excited about the concert too, but once again I'm getting a little tired of our lives revolving around *The Frozen* and their schedule.

Ten minutes goes by and Ryder still isn't back. Then fifteen minutes. At twenty minutes Deklan looks at his phone. "What's taking him so long?"

"Do you want me to go check on him?" I ask, ready to be out of the restaurant altogether and away from conversation about Gorge Days.

Deklan is easing up out of the bench, but Kenzie rests a hand on his arm and he sits back down. "If you want to."

I was only too ready to get out of the restaurant.

I half expect to run into Ryder as I walk back to the apartment. I pass by an old couple. The lady smiles and wishes me a good evening, and I am reminded how most people back home rarely made eye contact.

Life here just seems less harried, I suppose. Not everyone is in a rush to get where they're going and that's a welcome change.

I walk up the steps toward the apartment.

The apartment door is partially open. I walk in and nail Ryder in the face as he is walking out.

"Jesus, woman, are you trying to kill me?" he asks, holding his nose.

"Oh my God, are you bleeding?"

He touches his nose and sure enough, it comes back wet with blood.

I push past him to the kitchen and yank the roll of paper towels off the counter. I wet one and approach him.

Wary of me, he reaches out for it, but I push his hands aside.

"Put your head back," I order.

He does as I ask.

Along with blood coming from his right nostril, there is also a red line along the bridge of his nose.

"I'm so sorry, Ryder."

"You're apologizing entirely too much."

"I've been such a klutz lately."

"You mean you're normally not?" There is that smirk

again.

"No, I'm not a klutz." Well, that was kind of a lie. "I mean, I have my moments...except for when I am around certain individuals."

"Like me, you mean?"

I clear my throat. "Just around guys, I think."

"Who else makes you nervous?" he asks in that silky soft voice that makes the hair on my arms stand on end.

"You don't make me nervous."

He lifts his brows.

"Okay, well maybe you make me a *little* nervous. Let's face it, your reputation precedes you, so I think that's why I'm a bit apprehensive."

"Apprehensive, and yet I've grown on you, haven't I... despite your desire to hate me?"

"Maybe a little." I smile. "And for the record, I don't hate you."

I realize he's changed into track pants.

Following my gaze, he winces. "It was these or skinny jeans that I wear only for concerts."

"Only for concerts, huh?" I rub my hands together. "I can't wait to see that."

"The girls like to see the package, you know."

I could have done without hearing that. The comment makes me laugh though, and I shake my head. "Tell me you'll wear them at least once before I head home."

"I will. I promise." He slides his hands inside the track pants pockets.

Honestly, I think he looks smoking hot in them, but I won't tell him that. His ego doesn't need the added boost at the moment.

"Ange, I hate the thought of you leaving...despite the fact you were kind of a bitch when you first arrived."

"I wasn't a bitch. I mean, maybe I was kind of cold, but you had also hurt my best friend."

"Your best friend, who, need I remind you, is now

together with my best friend." His brows lift. "I managed to get myself played a bit in that relationship as well, so it's kind of a wash as far as I'm concerned."

"Fair enough," I say, and he puts an arm around my shoulders.

He lifts his head. "Does my nose look better?"

"There's just a little blood," I say, taking the paper towel and dabbing at the spot of dried blood. "You do have a red mark across the bridge though. Hopefully it won't bruise."

"It'll keep people guessing."

As always, he smells amazing. I have this strange desire to bury my head in his chest and inhale.

Overhead, it sounds like someone is dragging a heavy table across the floor.

"What are they doing up there?" I ask, looking at Ryder.

"Who knows? Maybe they're getting busy." He gives me a wink. "Apartment living. It's not without its downsides."

I completely ignore the innuendo about the neighbors and what could be happening up there and savor the hug a few more seconds before he locks the door behind us.

"So are we still on for a sleepover tonight?" he asks, a shit-eating grin on his lips.

"Yeah, I think so."

"You sleeping in my bed?"

The idea of sharing a bed with Ryder after last night's encounter with Cole is more than a little unnerving. "I'll probably stick to the couch."

"What if the apartment is haunted or something? You know that sound upstairs could have come from a ghost."

My stomach drops to my toes. "You're freaking me out."

"The building is old. I've heard stories."

I stare at him for a long moment and his expression doesn't falter. Oh my God, is he serious? I'd watched a lot of shows on television about old buildings being haunted. And we were just blocks away from Fort Vancouver.

Kenzie's apartment was old...but not as old as the

building. And all the features seemed to be original.

He laughs. "Nice, you're thinking about it, aren't you? My bed doesn't seem so bad now, does it?"

"Fine, but no touchy feely."

He puts both hands up, like a criminal who is surrendering. "Hey, I'll keep my hands to myself, I promise."

SEVENTEEN

A nge

Dinner goes well, and I relax but decide not to overeat. I had been gorging since I've been in Vancouver, and not having my mom around to remind me to chew each bite twenty-five times has been liberating in some ways, but my waistline is expanding by the day and my clothes are already getting tighter. The last thing I want to do when I arrive home is to have to invest in a new wardrobe.

We all walk back to the apartment and Brooke and Curtis stay around for an hour after dinner, and then the four of us are alone.

"I wish cable was set up," Deklan says, pouring a can of cola into a glass. "But the cable guy won't be here until Tuesday."

"You have a DVD player," Kenzie says, getting up and reaching into a box. She produces an old DVD player.

After a few minutes Deklan has it running. It seems like the only DVDs he owns are action flicks and surprisingly, a few older westerns. Ryder made a smartass comment about Deklan being a cowboy in a past life.

Midway into the second movie I start to drift off. I wake up to Ryder tickling the end of my nose.

I swipe at his finger and he laughs under his breath. The sound makes me even warmer and fuzzier.

Across the living room, Kenzie is facing Deklan, her back to the TV. She's passed out too.

"I'm tired," I say, and stand up and reach out to help Ryder up. After talking about haunted apartments, I'm not about to sleep on the couch tonight.

"Ready for bed?"

Deklan is already easing Kenzie up, and they head to his bedroom.

I follow Ryder to his room.

We find sheets for the queen sized bed and I'm soon crawling between the soft, flannel sheets.

"You want a t-shirt to sleep in?"

I glance down at my clothes and nod. "Sure."

He tosses me a soft, well-worn tee. "Turn around," I say, motioning for him to face the wall.

He immediately does as asked.

The shirt barely reaches my upper thighs. I quickly slide under the blankets, and he turns before I tell him he can.

The bed dips beneath Ryder's weight. "Good night."

"Good night," I say, and he turns the lamp off.

For someone who was exhausted minutes before, I am now fully awake. The apartment is quiet and I can hear myself breathe. It's almost too quiet, really.

I had never been great at sleeping in unfamiliar places. Granted, my best friend is in the same apartment, but right now that hardly helped.

I close my eyes. When I open them, a warm body is

wedged against me, spooning me. It takes me a second to orient myself, to remember where I am and who I'm with.

I reach for my phone. It's three a.m. and I have slept hard for three hours. I close my eyes but it is difficult to fall back to sleep, especially with Ryder's hand resting on my waist.

I roll over and face him. He doesn't budge.

The light from the phone gives off a little light, and I stare at him in the golden glow. His features in sleep are as amazing as when he is awake. I like being able to look at him when he isn't aware, and it seems like Ryder is always aware.

Despite my efforts not to like Ryder, I find that I do. In fact, I like him more with every day that passes. He has this way of making me forget about my troubles. Granted, having Cole aka the man of my desires like me and show me how much he liked me by dry humping me is hardly a catastrophe. Yet I'm let down. For five years I've adored him from afar and thought up every scenario and fantasy possible. I feel kind of like I did as a kid when I realized there was no such thing as Santa.

With a sigh, I snuggle closer to Ryder and close my eyes.

R^{yder}

I wake to the sound of honking outside my bedroom window.

I cover my head with a pillow and turn to find myself face to face with a pretty girl.

Ange is flat on her back, one arm flung over her head, the other out to her side. The comforter just barely covers her toned stomach where my tee-shirt has ridden up.

I tug a little at the comforter, and instinctively, she pulls the cover up to her chin.

Damn. I smile to myself and slide out of bed.

She doesn't move a muscle.

When I open the door I see Deklan standing by the window, staring out. He turns and looks at me. There's no welcoming smile, or even a nod. In his hand he's holding a coffee cup.

I glance at the clock. "It's only ten thirty and you look like you're ready to choke someone."

"Can I talk to you?"

My stomach tightens. I know that tone, and I can see he's serious by his expression.

"What's up?"

"You know that girl from the concert the other night? Amber…the one you had the little fling with in the closet?"

"Yeah, I know who you're talking about. What about her?"

"Well, apparently she dropped by the shop late last night." He walks to the kitchen counter and slides an envelope toward me. The flap is unopened and I don't have to ask Deklan if he's looked inside. "She said she wanted to give you a little something. She says she owed you from the other night when you overpaid her."

I frown. Overpaid her?

He opens the envelope. There's a small baggie of pills staring back at me.

My heart drops to my toes.

Fuck.

Fuck.

Fuck!

I open my mouth and no words come out. The look on Deklan's face kills me.

"How long have you been using?"

I swallow past the lump in my throat. I shake my head. "I'm not…"

"Don't fucking lie to me!" He crushes the baggie in his fist. I rarely see Deklan lose control, and he's at the brink. His fists are white and I know he wants to choke me.

I take a deep breath and release it. "A few days."

He sucks the lip-ring into his mouth and chews on it. "So you were using when the band confronted you the other night…and you lied and said you were clean."

It wasn't a question.

I nod.

He shakes his head and runs a hand through his hair. "Jesus Christ, Ryder, they trusted you. *I* trusted you."

"I'm sorry, Deklan. It's just a few Xanax's a day."

"Dude, you're lying. I had a gut feeling you were then, but I wanted to believe you when you looked me in the eye and told me you were straight."

I feel like the world's biggest asshole.

"Curtis has been on me to have you tested, but I told him with the move to lay off you."

"I'm trying, Deklan. I only took a Xanax yesterday… just to take off the edge."

Long minutes pass as he watched me watch him. I hear the ticking of the clock on the wall behind me, as though the second hand is pounding out the rhythm of my fate.

It takes a hell of a lot for Deklan to get mad at me, and it is very clear he is pissed off now.

He sets his cup down. "You're out of the band, Ryder."

A fist to the gut would have been easier to take. "But Gorge Days is coming up."

"You knew the rules. They apply to everyone. No one is exempt. You know that, Ryder."

I hate how he uses my name every time he speaks. I feel like a kid being chastised by a parent.

"Just keep it on the down low until after Gorge Days. I swear I'll stop right this second."

"You know I can't do that. I've spent too long building this band, and there were rules when you started." Deklan takes a step closer and his expression softens. "Maybe you should try rehab? There are some great facilities here locally. I have savings, and I'll gladly pay—"

"No!"

He looks like I'd slapped him.

"You've been saving all this time for a house, and I'm not going to take your money from you. You've helped me enough as it is." I want to cry my eyes out, but the bitch is I have only myself to blame. "I don't need rehab. I've got this. I do. Dude, it was just a few pills."

"There's no such thing as just a few pills when you're an addict."

Wow, that was harsh…

Releasing a long, drawn-out breath, Deklan shakes his head, grabs his coat off the back of the chair, and starts for the door. "I need some air."

"Do you want me to leave?"

"Where would you go?" He sounds as exasperated as he looks.

The only place I could think of going was my grandparents' house…and they were still disappointed with me. I hadn't been the best houseguest, and I'd taken advantage of their kindness.

The door slams shut behind Deklan.

I never thought I would see the day when even Deklan got tired of my bullshit.

I catch sight of myself in the mirror. All the signs of my drug use are there. I had lost weight, my eyes are red and I have dark circles beneath them. "You're a fucking idiot," I say to my reflection, and it's all I can do not to punch the mirror.

EIGHTEEN

A^{nge}

"How much longer are you in town for?"

Payton's question is directed at me, and unfortunately, I am mid-bite.

With all eyes on me, I swallow the mouthful of cheeseburger and wipe my hands on the napkin. "A few more weeks."

My mother would be appalled.

Melissa had asked Payton a ton of questions and seemed to be pleased with all the answers. Payton's parents were both doctors—her mom an anesthesiologist and her dad a brain surgeon.

Her farts probably smelled like roses, too.

I wish more than anything that she would just leave already. That, or I wish Cole would leave. His absence will make my life a lot less complicated, that's for sure.

I am a bumbling mass of confusion.

I continue stuffing my face and thankfully Payton is in mid-discussion with Melissa about an article she read online this morning about healthcare.

Cole pushes his food around his plate and I feel his gaze settle on me.

I completely ignore him.

A few more questions are directed my way about my family, and I can tell Payton's digging. Why does she care so much, or is she just trying to be polite by acting interested in my life?

Cole sets his fork down and clears his throat. "There's a plaza in Bel Air named after Ange's great grandfather. The man's a wizard in the industry and her family is extremely well respected."

Wow, I hadn't expected that, nor had Payton apparently. Her brow is slightly arched as she stares at me. Maybe she has a strong intuition and senses that Cole and I had been more than just friends.

She shouldn't worry. I had absolutely no intention of letting what happened the other night with Cole happen again. There was just no way, especially with Payton hanging around.

However, I was actually really excited to see Ryder again. Aside from him spooning me last night during the sleepover, he hadn't touched me and seemed content to just snuggle. I had slept amazingly well, too. When I woke up, he had left and I'd been disappointed. Deklan said he had an errand to run, but in my mind I wondered if he'd left intentionally.

Now I was just being paranoid.

I liked Ryder and I liked Cole.

But now Payton was in the picture.

I had liked Cole for so long that it was impossible to turn that off completely overnight, and yet I had such a sense of disappointment with him. Maybe because I had expected him to be different, and to actually behave in a way like Ryder had treated me these past few days.

Oh, the irony that they were both exactly the opposite of what I thought they would be.

I felt stupid, but most of all, I hate that Cole lied to me. I did, and I had always been one of those people who believed the best in everyone. This year it seems like my reality had been ripped out from underneath me…and it hadn't come so much by way of my own family, because they were their same boring selves. I had learned so much from watching Kenzie and her life, and experiencing what she'd gone through…granted, from a third-party perspective, and yet I had felt that pain, felt the sword in my side like I had been the one who had been betrayed by a beloved parent.

All the things Kenzie had told me about Ryder had been the same with her brother. Even more, Cole had a girlfriend—someone he had failed to say anything about, even after kissing me. He would have slept with me and then what? Would he have told me about her later?

Oh my God, was I one of those people who would never be good enough?

And I almost pitied Payton. She hangs on to his every word and laughs at everything he says. Once during dinner, she actually lifts her napkin to her lips, licks it, and wipes barbecue sauce off the side of his face.

He brushes her hand away, and she looks at him, brows furrowed. "It never bothered you before when I did that."

They kiss a few times, short, awkward kisses, and while Melissa beams, Kenzie squeezes my hand beneath the table. I flash her a reassuring smile. Cole looks confused by my reaction.

I had dodged a bullet. That's how I look at it now. I am grateful that maybe things had played out how they had with us grinding on each other with our clothes on. It could have been a completely different outcome and I would feel far worse than I did now.

My phone goes off and Ryder's face appears on the screen.

All eyes are on me.

"Sorry," I say, and pick up the phone.

The text message is from Ryder. "Walk with me?" it reads

My heart actually skips a beat.

A second later, there is a knock at the door.

"Is that Ryder?" Kenzie says, pushing her chair back.

Sure enough, Ryder is standing at the door. Seeing us sitting around the dinner table, his eyes widen. "I'm sorry, I didn't realize you were having dinner. Should I come back?"

"Of course not," Melissa says. "Are you hungry, Ryder?"

"No, thank you. Deklan and I had Chinese before he went to practice." His gaze settles on me. "I was wondering if you wanted to go for a walk."

"Sure…if it's alright with you, Melissa?"

She beams and even gives me a wink. "Of course it's okay." Apparently she doesn't have any hard feelings toward Ryder.

"Do you want to come with us, Kenzie?" I ask, holding my breath.

"No, you two go ahead," she says with a soft smile. "I have a phone call to make."

No doubt to Deklan.

Cole stands abruptly and starts clearing the table. I feel his gaze on me as he watches us walk out the door and down the front steps.

Ryder is quiet. Neither of us says a word as we cross the street.

We walk a city block before he glances at me and takes my hand. "I want to thank you, Ange."

I brush my thumb along his. "Thank me? For what?"

"For being there for me when I needed someone. You've been a good friend and I sincerely appreciate that."

I notice that his hand is shaking. I squeeze it. "Are you

okay?"

"No, not really."

"What's wrong?" I ask, pulling him toward a short retaining wall. I sit down and he joins me.

Last night he'd been the one to ask about my problems. Now I want to be there for him.

He opens his mouth but hesitates. "A friend of mine came by the shop yesterday and gave Deklan some pills that she said belonged to me."

"But you don't take pills. You've been clean for weeks."

He takes a deep breath and releases it in a sigh. "I had been clean for almost two weeks, but then the night at the Roxbury I took pills."

"So you were using when the band confronted you?"

Again, he hesitates and I have my answer.

He runs his hands through his hair. "Everyone is going to hate me."

"No, they won't."

"Deklan is pissed. I looked him in the eye and I lied to him. I was just too afraid to say anything to them, especially when I was being told I'd be cut from the band. We've waited forever to get the Gorge Days gig, and I can't deal with being cut again, especially when I'm struggling to stay clean."

Kenzie had told me about how it had been for Ryder before, and how everyone had managed to get clean but him.

Of course I feel disappointed by the news, but I also respect him for telling me.

"Do Brooke and Curtis know?"

"Not yet. Deklan told me it was up to me to come clean, so that's what I'm going to do. I just wanted to talk to you first."

I am strangely moved by that.

"I can do this, Ange. I know I can. I did it before. I can do it again. I just hope it's not too late, and that the guys will let me back in the band before Gorge Days."

"How long will it take to pee clean?"

"Three to four days maybe?"

"I'll do what I can to help you. My mom is completely into holistic medicine. She's tried everything from naturopathic medicine to cure arthritis to acupuncture and massage. Some people think it's crap, but honestly—it works."

I can see the hope in his eyes, and it makes me feel better to know that I can help.

"I'm happy to help you in any way I can, Ryder. This is serious, but I know you can do it."

I slide my hand around his elbow and he smiles. "Maybe you can spend the night again with me soon. Like tonight?"

"I can't tonight."

"Why? Does Cole want you home?"

He sounds almost jealous…and I'm surprised by that.

I frown, even if I'm a little encouraged by the fact he might be jealous. "Of course he doesn't want me home. He has his girlfriend."

"He doesn't like me."

"Maybe he's threatened by you." I think most men are intimidated by Ryder.

"Should he be threatened by me?" he asks, and I can feel my heart pounding in my ears. "Do you have feelings for me, Ange?"

Ryder

I hold my breath as I await Ange's answer.

The sides of her mouth quirk. "Yes."

I half expect her to say no, that she feels nothing for me. That her Neanderthal of a boyfriend who she'd been crushing on since she was a girl still had her heart, even after introducing his girlfriend to her.

But she has feelings for me. Me, prescription drug abuser me. Drug addict me. I've become so used to being looked down upon by everyone around me—family, close friends, and even acquaintances who had heard of Brooke's overdose, that the last person I had expected to still have my back was a girl who I thought would judge me harsher than anyone else.

She continues to surprise me...in all the best ways.

I reach out and take hold of her hand.

She grins at me. "I want to help you, Ryder. You're stronger than you know."

"Thanks, and you're not the ice queen I thought you were."

She hits me playfully on the arm. "Me? An ice queen? Now that's a first. I'll have you know I received the award for most welcoming student at Saint Catherine's three years in a row."

"Wow, how impressive." And to think that all this time I thought I had her all figured out, I realize how far off base I had been.

She had a heart of gold. Here she was ready to throw me a lifeline when everyone else in my life had pretty much bailed and given up on me. Well, Deklan hadn't given up on me, but he was tired...and I honestly didn't blame him. I could exhaust anyone. Hell, I exhausted myself.

"Ryder, you'll be alright. We'll get you help, but will you promise me something?"

My heart misses a beat. I didn't like making promises to anyone, because I rarely, if ever, delivered.

"If you try the different holistic remedies and it doesn't work for you—will you go to an in-patient rehab facility?

I stare into her beautiful green eyes. I could have promised her anything just to get her off my ass. The thing is, I need someone who is willing to push me, and to help me, and to make me believe that I can get clean if I really want to.

And the thing is...I really want to.

I need a new direction. I want more than being a front

desk clerk and assistant at *Branded*. First step, I need to get clean.

Ange rests her head against my shoulder. "I believe in you, Ryder. Now you just have to believe in yourself."

NINETEEN

R^{yder}

The knocking at the door won't stop.

At first I wonder if Deklan has locked himself out, then remember that he's stashed a key. He'd said he had errands to run and would be back before dinner.

Maybe Ange or Kenzie? No, they were having a family potluck over at Brooke's house.

I bury my head under my pillow and wait for the person to go away.

They don't.

Instead, the knocking continues and grows louder by the second.

Maybe Deklan has misplaced the stash key.

That, or a neighbor is being a dick. Great, just what I needed on top of everything else.

I pull my jeans on and walk toward the door.

Taking a look in the mirror, I run a hand through my hair and yank the door open.

My mother's frown pierces my soul.

She is the last person I expect to come knocking at my door.

"Joshua."

Aside from my grandmother and teachers, she's the only person who calls me by my given name.

Her gaze shifts slowly over my body and back up again, coming to a stop at the tattoo on my upper arm. "Oh, you didn't." The disgust and disappointment is evident in her expression and voice.

"Good morning to you too, Mom."

"Actually, it's afternoon." She flashes a too tight smile my way while she gazes past me. She's dying to get in, no doubt so she can inspect and tell me everything that is wrong with the place.

"It has come to my attention that you have fallen off the wagon…again."

Who the hell would have told her that?

"I've been clean for two days. Actually, almost three."

"Oh wow, Joshua. Three whole days. Perhaps I should buy you a medal. Seventy-two hours without abusing your body with narcotics. What an amazing accomplishment."

"Thanks for the encouragement." I try to remember the years when she wasn't a sarcastic, keeping up with the Joneses cold bitch. She had been kind at one time, right? It hadn't been my drug-addled mind just wishing it to make me feel better.

Her eyelids close and she takes a long, steadying breath. "I do not understand what happened in your life that makes you think you need to take drugs to get through a day. My God, Joshua…you didn't even make it two weeks without using again."

I feel a sense of anger toward whomever it was who had told her this information. What the hell?

"Please tell me what it is that is so tough about your life that you feel you must use narcotics?" She actually taps her foot. "Hmmm?"

Part of it might be my unfeeling, insensitive mother who cares more about her status in the community than her own family. How badly I want to say the words, but I don't want to deal with the tirade that would follow.

Not wanting my neighbors to be privy to our conversation, I ask, "Do you want to come in?"

She hesitates and glances past me into the hallway once more. She's not fooling me for a second.

"I'm alone."

Staring at my tattoo, she passes by me, muttering something unintelligible under her breath.

I offer her a seat on the couch and excuse myself long enough to put on a t-shirt, brush my teeth, and wash my face. When I walk into the room, she's examining a picture of Kenzie and Deklan that had been taken at the county fair just weeks before. "A beautiful girl."

"Yes, she is." I grab the coffee pot out of the cradle and fill it with water. "Would you like some coffee?"

She sets the picture back down and crosses her arms over her chest.

"No, thank you."

I set the coffee pot in the sink and instead grab a bottle of water out of the fridge, and again, offer her one.

She shakes her head.

"Your father suggested I drop by and see you. We have options for you."

How typical that my father would have ideas, but it would be my mother to deliver the news. Some things never changed, and in my household they never would. My mother wore the pants in the family.

Not waiting for me to ask what the plans were, she continues. "There is a rehabilitation facility in Bellingham that we have checked into and it takes your father's insurance plan."

"Bellingham. Isn't that like five hours away?"

"Four, actually. Your father and I both feel that being around Vancouver and your friends would make it difficult for your recovery."

"My friends aren't the problem. *I'm* the problem, Mom."

"Be that as it may, Joshua, we feel it would be easiest for you to recover at a location *away* from Vancouver. You don't need the temptation of getting in a car and driving a couple of hours to get here. That's just plain dangerous and out of the question."

"I want to be near family and friends. This is home. This is where I need to be to recover."

She sniffs. "Out of the question."

Once again she isn't listening to a word I say.

"I don't need rehab anyway. I'm going to—"

"You were kicked out of your band yet again, Joshua. You are burning bridges. How will you get through life if you continually expect everyone to just look the other way whenever you do something wrong?"

"Burning bridges?"

"Yes, Joshua. You are burning bridges. Do you not realize that?"

Just her tone has me on edge. In fact, I am shaking and she knows it. She glances at my hand. I clench my fist and force myself to calm down. "How is it that you seem to know so much about what's happening in my life?"

She actually shifts on her feet but keeps her gaze steady. "I dropped by the home where you had been living with Deklan and spoke to Curtis. My goodness, that boy's hair is horrendous. I can only imagine how difficult it is to clean those—what is it that you call them—dreadlocks." She shakes her head. "Anyway, he told me you had moved out with Deklan and seemed shocked you had not told me. I am surprised by Deklan as well. Normally he keeps me apprised of everything."

I feel a huge sense of relief knowing the information had come by way of Curtis and not Deklan.

"I'm getting clean, Mom." It isn't a lie. I haven't had drugs since the day before yesterday, and now, after her visit, I am even more determined to get clean.

"We've heard that before, Joshua."

"Thanks for your visit, Mom." I stand and take a controlling breath. "I have work today."

"At the tattoo parlor downstairs?" She lifts her brow. "Soon I'm sure you'll be covered with them…just like your best friend. I adore Deklan. You know I do, but what compels a person to cover themselves in ink?" She gives a shudder. "Repulsive."

Get the fuck out. I want to scream the words. Instead, I walk toward the door, giving her no choice but to follow me.

"I don't think you understand. Your father and I have already put a deposit down on the facility in Bellingham—"

"Mom, I didn't ask for your help with this. In fact, you told me to get out of your house until I could piss clean."

She lifts her chin two inches. "I'm teaching you responsibility, Joshua."

I have a dozen retorts and yet I keep my mouth shut. She is brimming with anger and I wonder why. What happened in her life that she's so fucking miserable, that even now, when she is facing her oldest son, she can show so little emotion?

My heart is pounding so hard, I'm surprised it's not flying right out of my chest. "I appreciate the offer. I honestly do…but I'm doing this my way. Deklan is helping, and so is my band, and Kenzie and Ange."

She frowns. "Who is Ange?"

"A really great girl," I say, wishing she were here right now. "Someone you would actually approve of." Most of all because she came from money and my mom was all about the money. "And she's taking me for some holistic treatments."

"Holistic?" Her brow lifts, along with the side of her

lip. "Honestly, honey. I think you're bound for failure. You'll never do it alone."

"Thanks for the vote of confidence, Mom."

"If we can't get the money refunded, I'll be adding it to the list of money you owe your father and I."

"What list?"

She had a list of the money I had borrowed through my life? Hell, I had just graduated from high school. "Never mind."

She scrunches her nose. "Is that mildew I smell?"

"It's an older building. I love it here."

"How can you afford it…or dare I ask?"

"I'm working for rent." Granted, Deklan paid the majority of all the bills right now, but I was doing my best to pay him back, and I was determined to pay him back. "I have a job."

"No college then?"

"Maybe one day."

Clearing her throat, she gives me a bored look. "You'll probably be hearing from your father."

"He can call me anytime, Mom."

I half expect her to say her door would be open at any time, but there was no talk about me coming home. Not that I want to. It's just sobering to know that this is how things with my mom would end.

What if I'd been a truly awful kid? It's not like I hadn't done my part around the house. I'd spent a decade mowing the yard every Saturday. Well, before Deklan had arrived on the scene and taken over most of the chores.

She brushes a lock of my hair behind my ear. "Your hair is getting too long, dear. You look scruffy."

Her touch feels foreign to me. She had never been a hugger or overly affectionate. My grandma's hugs—now you felt the love. No one hugged like her. Just thinking of my grandma made me realize how much I had disappointed her …and everyone else who loved and cared about me.

I had a lot of making up to do.

"Well, goodbye, Joshua."

"Goodbye, Mom," I say to her retreating back.

I close the door and stand with my head against the wood, listening until her steps fade in the distance. She feels like a stranger to me.

If my own mother didn't believe in me and my ability to get clean without a rehab center, then it was up to me to change everyone's mind.

I pick up my phone and call Ange.

She doesn't answer, and I immediately wonder if she is out with Cole. After all, Payton left first thing today to head home.

I also wonder what had happened the other night after I walked her home. She had been honest to me about Cole—how they had fooled around, and how she had felt guilty about it afterward. I'd had to grit my teeth when I thought about how he'd used her, and then I thought of all the women who would like to have their boyfriends beat the shit out of me.

Maybe it was karma for all the crap I had pulled in my time.

All I know is that I feel like a better person because Ange is in my life. Seeing things through her eyes gives me a better perspective of what I want. She knows what she wants, and she is determined to go after it.

And her parents…they sound a bit obnoxious and completely anal about controlling her life, but then again, I wonder what it would feel like to have someone care so much that they were determined to give you the best life possible.

I sit in the nearest chair and finish off the water. In the past forty-eight hours I've heard and seen my family and my best friend on the planet tell me I need help.

Ange had said she'd help.

I punch in her phone number and send a text.

Me: I NEED YOUR HELP!

The phone immediately rings. "Ryder, are you okay?"

My throat is tight. "Not really."

"Are you at home?"

I hear the alarm in her voice, and in the background I hear Kenzie. I've scared them and that wasn't my intention. "Yes. I just…you know that offer to help me. The things your mom did to help her with sleeping."

"Yes."

"I'd like to try something that might take the edge off."

"I'll be there in forty-five minutes, okay?"

Within two minutes, the phone rings and it's Deklan. "Ryder, what's going on?"

Of course Kenzie would call him.

Oddly, just hearing his voice makes me want to cry. "My mom dropped by."

"What did she want?"

"She said she reserved a place at a rehab center for me."

He's silent for a second. "Rehab…where?"

"In Bellingham."

"What? Why Bellingham? You'd be so far away."

"I told her I wouldn't go. I mean, I can't."

"It's okay, Ryder. I'll be there in ten. I'm over at Mr. Cavendish's."

That's right. He had told me the old neighbor had been after him to move a couple of plants from the front yard to the back. Always good on his word, Deklan had followed through.

Just like he always did.

"Don't worry about it. Ange will be here in a few."

"I don't want you alone."

I smile, grateful I have him in my life. "Deklan, I'm okay. I swear."

There's another long pause. "I'm almost done. Why don't you wait there with Ange until I get back, and we can go together."

Tears roll down my cheeks and I wipe them away with the back of my hand. He's the best man I know, and I've been a complete asshole to him.

Oh my God, I fucking need help. I'm desperate for it. This is something I can't just snap my fingers at to make it go away, but I need it to. "I'm alright. I'm going to take a shower and go off with Ange."

"You sure?"

"I'm sure. Thanks, Deklan."

TWENTY

A nge

I take the steps to Ryder's apartment two at a time, and when he meets me at the door I'm surprised to find him looking okay. I hadn't known what to expect when I'd received that text, and then hearing his voice. He hadn't sounded right.

Behind me, Kenzie actually breathes a sigh of relief.

"Just the person I wanted to see."

"Really?"

"I have something planned for us," I say, and Ryder's eyes immediately light up.

"I'm all yours."

"Bring a suit."

He frowns. "We're going swimming?"

I grin. "You'll see."

"Deklan wants me to stay here and wait for him,"

Kenzie interjects.

"Sounds good. We'll see you when we get back," I say, and taking Ryder by the hand we head toward his car.

He tosses me the keys. "You drive."

I don't know if that's the smartest idea, given the fact I've never driven in Portland before, and particularly downtown Portland, but I'm not about to argue with him.

I get into the driver's side of his car, put on my seatbelt, and turn the engine on. His mind is somewhere else already. He's spacing off, biting his lip and staring at the dash. I want to ask him what had happened to make him call me, but I don't want to pry. He was reaching out to me and that was enough.

"You'll have to help me with directions."

I focus on making sure I don't drive down the one-way roads that are so prominent in every downtown area. Vancouver is no exception. I cut a lady off and she lays on her horn.

I wince and Ryder laughs under his breath.

"You sure you don't want to drive?" I ask.

He shakes his head. "Nope, you're doing great."

My mom hated driving so much that she had hired a chauffeur…until my father had given her an ultimatum and told her it was the chauffeur or the cook. She couldn't have both.

The cook had won out. Thank goodness, because my mom couldn't boil water. At least that's what my dad said.

"How do I get to Southbound I-5?" I ask, hoping I was headed in the right direction.

"You'll want to be in the right-hand lane," he says, motioning to the upcoming light.

I signal and pull into the right-hand lane.

I feel Ryder watching me.

I glance at him and lift a brow. "What?"

"So what happened last night with Cole?"

It's a question I sort of expected, especially after he'd

already asked me about Cole yesterday.

I can feel my cheeks flush. "Nothing. I mean, he's with Payton and the truth is they're good together."

"Are you sad?"

"I don't know." I shrug. "Maybe a little. I did like him for what seemed like forever."

His silence unnerves me a little.

"I'm more concerned about us remaining friends, you know?"

He nods but doesn't say anything.

"I'm just glad I didn't sleep with him." I was surprised to have said the words aloud. Damn, my nervousness had gotten the best of me again and I'd rambled.

"Are you?" He looks relieved.

"Most definitely."

Ryder flashes a wolfish smile that makes my heart miss a beat. "I think old Cole will always think of you as the one that got away."

I frown. "Not likely."

"Trust me, every guy has that one girl that got away."

I remember how Ryder had looked at Kenzie when I'd first arrived in Vancouver, and how I always thought I'd seen regret there. I wasn't about to ask him if Kenzie had been the one that had gotten away for him.

"You seem to like everyone, Ange. Even Payton won you over. How does that work?"

"I don't like everyone," I say. "For instance, that girl you kept sneaking off with after your concerts got under my skin. Trust me, the two of us will never be friends."

He actually snorts. "I don't even remember her name."

"Amber," I blurt.

He lifts his brows and smiles.

That is until a Hyundai with a huge dent in its side swerves into my lane. I am able to slide into the left lane before we collide. I lay on the horn and give the punk kid in the car the finger.

Ryder puts his hand over mine and squeezes. "Calm down, girl. You're going to get us both in trouble if you're not careful."

Oh my God, is he serious?

I realize he isn't as he starts to laugh.

"Focus," he suggests, and I do focus for the next fifteen minutes that takes us closer to the city center. There are at least four bridges we have to cross to get to our location. Maybe I should have actually located the place on a map before I had committed to it.

It will be so worth it once we get there, I tell myself as we cross over the highest of the bridges.

Downtown Portland is alive with activity. I overshoot the shop I'm looking for twice before I find a parking spot and parallel park the car like a pro. "Here we are!"

Ryder looks up the city block. "Where are we going?"

I give him a wink. "You'll see."

What awaits us inside the Cloud Nine Spa is a sterile looking waiting room. Everything is white. Bright white and chrome, which isn't exactly the warm welcoming vibe I was hoping for. I want Ryder to be excited about this experience, not be terrified that he was going in for a medical procedure.

A gorgeous redhead with enormous fake boobs walks out from behind a curtain, clipboard in hand. Of course, just my luck…

"Good afternoon," she says, giving us both a welcoming smile. "Welcome to Cloud Nine Spa. My name is Sienna. Are you both going in?" she asks.

I nod and look at Ryder. "Yes, unless you want to go alone."

"I don't know what this is, so I think it's safe to say I'm okay with you coming along for the ride."

Sienna glances at me, then hands me a clipboard. "I'll be right back with another form."

"Trust me, you'll love it."

"Have you done this before?" Ryder asks.

"I've done something similar."

"Of course you have," Ryder says in a silky soft voice.

"And forgive my bad manners," Sienna says when she returns with the extra clipboard. She is all business as she asks us to fill out paperwork.

When we finish, she asks both Ryder and me to follow her down a hallway into a room where a water feature gives off a nice sound. "Change into your swimsuits. There are robes there, and when you're done, meet me in the hallway."

I hurry up and remove my clothes and scurry into my bikini. I meet Ryder in the hallway. Where I have my towel wrapped tight around my body, his is hanging loosely around his neck.

"Now what?" Ryder asks, looking amused.

"We're going in a float tank."

He gives me a questioning look.

"You'll see…"

Karen steps in with her little promotional spiel about the benefits of the floating pods.

"I'm ready," Ryder says, rubbing his hands together.

After putting our belongings in storage baskets, we step into a giant looking egg. "The water wasn't hot tub hot, but comfortable. The salts in the water make it so that you float, so don't worry about becoming so comfortable that you'll drown," Sienna says. "Just allow the water to cradle you, relax, and the pod will dim on its own."

The water is only a couple of feet deep. I sit down and Ryder does the same, and we both ease onto our backs.

"Relax," I say, mostly to myself than to him.

"Enjoy!" Sienna says, before shutting the door.

We say nothing to each other, until the light dims and then slowly goes pitch-black.

I reach for Ryder's hand. My fingers slide through his and I give it a squeeze. In this weightless space I can almost feel his pain…and I want to take it away.

He needs me, and that's not a situation I have found

myself in too many times in my life. I feel honored and humbled that he had called me out of everyone he knew. If we needed to try a hundred different holistic treatments, then that's what we'd do.

And I was glad I could provide that for him. I thought about my time in Washington and how much fun I'd had, and how many more great days we would have before I left. I was determined that we would get Ryder over the hump before I boarded that plane for San Diego.

When the light in the room turns back on an hour later, we look at each other and smile.

"You're amazing, you know that?" Ryder says, and the expression on his face surprises me.

Slightly uncomfortable, I laugh, and it's obviously not the response he'd been expecting because he frowns.

Stepping out of the chamber, Ryder pulls me toward him. He cups my face with his hands and kisses me.

Goose bumps cover my flesh, and it's not from the cold air.

"Thank you," he whispers against my lips.

I put my hands over his and pull away just enough to look into his eyes. "You're welcome."

Sienna knocks and opens the door a second later, and we pull away from each other.

"How do you feel?" she asks, her eyes bright as she looks from me to Ryder and back again.

"Amazing," we say at the exact same time.

I brush my hair out and put it in a braid, smiling at the memory of Ryder braiding it not so long ago. I remembered how even back then his touch had done strange things to me.

The boy had magic fingers.

On the way home we talk about our experience in the tank and the strange calm that both of us had felt. There had been a funny moment when he'd admitted to ripping a fart, and I shook my head and laughed.

All in all, I hope more than anything that the floating pod had helped him forget about his addiction and what had been bothering him when he had called me.

"Stay with me tonight?" he asks when I pull up alongside his apartment.

He's waiting for my reply.

Of course I would stay, especially after the kind of day he'd had. "Sure."

I could tell by his expression that he had expected me to say no, but was thrilled I'd said yes.

I turn the ignition off and reach for the door but he stops me by leaning over and reaching for my hand. "Thank you for today. You were a real lifeline and I needed that. I needed you."

My insides tightened. I had never seen him so intense before.

"You're welcome." I smile. "It was fun."

He nods. "It was. I'd like to do it again sometime before you go."

Talk of me returning to San Diego just made me depressed. "Definitely."

We walk into the apartment and are both surprised to see Brooke and Curtis. I feel a little bit of tension between Ryder and Curtis, and wonder what that's about.

There's part of a sub sandwich on the counter that Curtis offers to us. I decline, but Ryder takes a piece and sets it on a plate.

"The manager from Gorge Days called," Curtis says melodramatically, dipping a chip into French Onion dip. "We have a suite lined up for us. It sleeps eight people, and there's room for us to store our equipment."

Ryder's shoulders straighten.

"I'm sure it will all be fine," Deklan says, changing the television channel.

"I think we should leave on Thursday instead of Friday though," Brooke adds. "Traffic is supposed to be horrendous."

I shift in my seat. What a bunch of insufferable assholes to be talking about Gorge Days in front of Ryder, especially when they knew how bummed out he is that he won't be a part of it.

I am in the kitchen with Kenzie making guacamole. She smiles reassuringly.

Kenzie had told me that Alec, the shrimp, had been practicing with them the past couple of days. If anyone brings up the kid's name tonight, I swear I will choke them.

"We should take two cars," Curtis says. "Don't you think, Dek?"

Deklan nods.

I can read Deklan like a book. He is so uncomfortable and obviously worried about Ryder's reaction.

"Are you getting a permission slip from Alec's mother?" I can't resist asking.

Ryder laughs under his breath, and yet I see pain in his eyes.

Damn, why hadn't I just kept my mouth shut?

Brooke frowns at me. "What is that supposed to mean?"

"He can't be thirteen."

"He's almost seventeen."

"No kidding," I say, stunned by the declaration.

"He's good," Brooke says defensively. "He knows every song we play, and he can sing well, too."

"Yeah, but he's no Ryder." This comes from Kenzie. She glances at Deklan and then the others. She shrugs. "It's the truth."

Deklan nods and looks pleased at his woman's declaration. "I agree."

Ryder smiles and I could tell he needed that little boost of confidence.

"You know I was wondering…do you think you can pass a drug test right now?" Brooke asks. There's hope in her voice. It's obvious she wants Ryder playing with them at Gorge Days.

"Yes, I can." He sounds incredibly confident.

"We don't have a drug test." Deklan mentions the obvious.

Brooke shrugs. "Yeah, but the pharmacy on the corner is open."

Deklan hands us cash and we're out the door and back with the test within ten minutes.

I can tell Ryder is nervous, which makes me nervous. I didn't know how long certain drugs stayed in the body.

Brooke hands the test to Deklan. "Go with him."

"You going to hold my dick for me?" Ryder asks, trying to make light of the situation. It works because everyone laughs.

R yder

We walk into the bathroom and Deklan hands me the cup. "You don't have to if you don't want to."

"You make it sound like you're going to fuck me."

He actually smiles at that. "Knock it off."

"Relax, bro. It's going to be okay."

"Shouldn't I be the one reassuring you?" he says.

I unzip my pants, piss in the cup and hand it to him.

He reads the directions aloud twice, and then takes the test card and slides it into the cup. Using the counter on his phone, he counts to fifteen before he removes the card and sets it on the counter.

"I'll bleach the counter when we're done," I say, finding humor to be better than stressing out about the results. So much relied on the next few minutes. I would either be playing with my band at the biggest gig of our career, or I would be watching from the audience.

"I want you to be there, regardless," Deklan says. He doesn't look at the card, but at me.

"I know. I want to be there too."

He nodded. "Tell me about the tank. It sounds bizarre."

"I think it's kind of like what floating in space would be like. Weightless, you know?"

Deklan nods.

"It's strange and beautiful at the same time. I actually saw like colors behind my eyelids. I don't know if I was just imagining it." I yammer on for minutes, just wanting the time to go by.

"It sounds incredible, and it seems to have helped. You're less on edge than when I talked to you earlier."

He was right. It had helped. He's given me an opening to talk about my mom's visit, but before I can say anything the phone alarm goes off.

I'm strangely calm as he compares the card to the corresponding information on the instructions. I can tell he goes over it a few times before he looks at me and grins. "It's negative. You're clean."

I smile. "Don't sound so surprised. I told you." I am so elated.

Card still in hand, he hugs me. "I love you, Ryder. You know that, right?"

I smile against his shoulder as I hug him back. It feels amazing to have someone care so much about me...who loves me unconditionally. "Yeah, I know it...and I love you, too."

"Come on, let's tell the others."

TWENTY-ONE

Ryder

The crowd at Gorge Days is crazy huge.

I can't believe the sea of people.

It is without a doubt the largest venue we'd ever played at, and word has it that some big names in the business are in the audience.

In the past week, our band has practiced for up to eight hours at a time. We are a well-oiled machine and I feel like I have a second lease on life.

Since Deklan had shown my band mates the drug test results, not one of them had questioned me about my sobriety. I had done a good faith drug test just last night, wanting, and I suppose needing in my own way to show them again that I was clean, and that I was determined to stay that way.

That I was determined to be a part of this band. Today,

I was going to give them all I had.

While Deklan and Curtis are messing with the amps on stage to prepare for our set, Brooke is pacing nervously back and forth backstage.

"You'll kill it," I say, and she comes up and gives me a big hug.

"I'm terrified."

Brooke had never been a big talker, and I wasn't necessarily either. I feel like I need to reassure her though.

"I know, but you've practiced for this day all your life."

"You've heard who's here?"

I nod. "Yeah, I know there are some heavy-hitters."

"What if we fuck it up?"

I grin. "What if we don't?"

She glances up at me with her big doe eyes. She *is* terrified.

"Play like there are no big talent scouts out there. Sing like you have done for every tiny college party we played at. Like you've done during every set in that fucking dungeon of a basement your boyfriend calls home."

She laughs under her breath. "Remember when we'd bring friends home from school to critique us?"

"Yeah, we even gave them score cards." I shake my head. "What a bunch of dumbasses we were."

"It just showed our dedication," Curtis says, coming up from behind us. He pulls Brooke away from me and into his arms. "Babe, you'll be amazing. Quit jonesing."

"Now I'd like to introduce to you a band from Vancouver, Washington!" the announcer says, and my nerves go into overload.

"At least they got our hometown right. They usually always say Portland," Brooke murmurs. Even now she can find something to complain about. I just have to smile, and oddly, I feel a strange desire to laugh.

I keep my cool about me though, reminding myself yet again how important the next thirty minutes is for us.

"Shhh." Curtis places a finger to her lips and Brooke playfully bites him.

"Without further ado, may I present *The Frozen*!" the announcer says.

The crowd comes back with a welcoming roar that sets my blood on fire.

"Let's go," Curtis says, already heading for the stage.

I hang back for a second. My heart pounds hard against my chest. I'm going out on that stage and I will play my heart out, not so much for myself, but for my band and for the people who trust me with their futures enough to give me another chance.

A hand slides around my shoulder. "You ready?"

I glance at Deklan. His green eyes are bright, shining with hope. He'd put this band together four years ago and he'd poured his heart and soul into it. "I am. You?"

"Definitely."

"Hey, thanks for everything, Dek. I couldn't have done it without you."

He grips my hand and we do our dorky handshake that we started as kids. Spreading his palm out, he displays the scar there. I do the same, and the matching white line reminds us of our bond. We had been kids when we'd cut each other's palms with the jackknife my grandpa had given me when I was seven. Blood brothers. We had vowed to each other years ago that we would always have each other's back, no matter what.

Deklan had proven true to his word. Time would never change that.

A whistle rents the air, and Deklan smiles. "Curtis's cue to get our asses out on stage."

"We are Kings," I say. The words were the phrase that Deklan and I had come up with to gain entry to our tree fort when we were kids. I don't think I had uttered those words since the tree fort had burned down the summer of my eighth grade year.

Deklan's lips quirk. He nods and gives me another quick hug. "We are Kings."

Ange

The energy of the crowd is electric.

Kenzie and I stand in the front of the enormous crowd, hoping that the bodyguards standing in front of us would offer some kind of protection against the crazy-ass crowd behind us.

I'm so nervous for the band I feel like I might hurl. I know Kenzie is the same way. Her hand is locked in my own.

Already people are jumping up and down yelling, "The Frozen, The Frozen, The Frozen."

The second Brooke and Curtis step out on stage, the crowd yells their approval.

Kenzie finally drops my hand and we both join in on the applause.

A minute goes by and still no Ryder and Deklan.

Curtis whistles, and a moment later Ryder and Deklan appear on stage.

The women in the crowd whistle and scream their approval. Kenzie and I look at each other and share a smile.

I don't know how my friend does it. I'm jealous and want to let everyone in the crowd know that I have a special relationship with this band, particularly the smoking hot bass player.

"Look at him," Kenzie says in approval of her man.

Deklan isn't wearing a shirt and his insanely shredded body looks amazing in low-riding dark jeans with the band of his boxers peeking out. He said he wanted to wear a sleeveless t-shirt at least, but Brooke, Kenzie, and I convinced him it would be good for the band if he showed his assets.

We listened to him yammer on for minutes about the quality of their playing and not having to fall back on anything other than their talent.

We all agreed with him and then hid his shirts.

Ryder is wearing a button-down sleeveless black shirt

that looks amazing. He's also wearing the skinny ass black jeans that I'd made fun of before when he'd told me about them, but I now completely understand the appeal. They left nothing to the imagination and were borderline obscene.

I love it.

Leather bracelets, dog-tag necklaces, and motorcycle boots complete the ensemble.

And in typical Ryder fashion, he plays the audience with style.

The crowd sings to the lyrics and I can see the joy in the band members' faces to have so many people know their song and sing them word for word. Kenzie and I sing right along with them. This is a moment in my life I know I will never forget, even when I am old. *The Frozen* sings five songs in total—one a new tune that Deklan had written for Kenzie.

We both cry our eyes out as Deklan's thoughts and feelings toward Kenzie were sung for everyone to hear. Brooke belts out the chorus, singing, "You've given me a reason for living. You're my peace, my soul, my everything. You're my peace, my soul, my everything."

I squeezed my friend's hand. I am grateful. Grateful she had brought me to Vancouver to spend the summer with her. Grateful that she had trusted me enough to share her fears with me, and grateful that she had introduced me to this beautiful group of people who I otherwise would have never had the opportunity to meet. I would have continued to be terrified of such experiences instead of throwing myself headfirst into just being and enjoying them for who they were…normal, flawed people who loved deeply, cared deeply, and made mistakes.

I will never look at the world the same way again.

The performance is flawless. They are pros, and they know they've done well when they take their final bow to thunderous applause and roars.

I give Kenzie a hug, and we make our way through the crowd toward the VIP area, to the area where huge white tents have been set up for the performers. Deklan, Ryder, Brooke, and Curtis have their backs to us. All are drinking water and sports drinks. We rush their way but stop when we notice the tall man with them. He wears a Rolex and designer clothing and looks like someone important. Deklan is doing most of the talking as the rest of the band just smile and nod their heads.

"Oh my God, do you think that's a scout?" Kenzie asks, her eyes huge.

I look at her and smile. "Yeah, I do."

TWENTY-TWO

Two months later…

I'd been called down to the school office fifteen minutes before the final bell rings. A thousand different scenarios are racing through my mind. My parents have never pulled me out early. Ever. I have to wonder what has happened. I check my phone. There are no messages.

I pull open the large wooden door that leads to the main office, a place that looks more like a posh hotel waiting room than a school reception area.

Sister Francis, a bird-faced nun, is sitting behind an oak desk. Seeing me, she approaches the main counter. "Your cousin is here for you, Angela. He's waiting in the parking lot."

"My cousin?"

"Yes, your cousin Joshua."

My stomach tightens. I readjust the strap of my

backpack and break eye contact. Sister Francis can pull a lie out of anyone, and she knows a fib when she sees it. Her narrowed eyes says she suspects Joshua is not a relative, and she's waiting for me to choke and tell her as much.

"I took the liberty of phoning your house. Although your mother was not available, your sister validated that she knew Joshua was coming to get you and that she would take responsibility should your parents question him about getting you out early."

It had to have been Stephanie. She had graduated from St. Catherine's last year and was at her first year in Pepperdine. She'd only been in college for a year and apparently was having a tough time cutting the cord because she came home every single weekend to stay with us.

Stephanie also knows how much I love Ryder. I'm crazy, head-over-heels in love with the gorgeous bad boy rocker. We had grown even closer since I had left Vancouver. We video chat every single day, texted when we didn't call, and some of those texts had gotten pretty sexy.

Sister Francis clears her throat loudly. "Carl is waiting to escort you."

"Okay, I'm ready."

If it wasn't for Carl, one of the school's security guards, I would run, but I'm forced to maintain control and keep pace with him.

It's been almost two months since I've seen Ryder in the flesh. The entire band was in Los Angeles to record their first CD with their new label.

The label they had signed on with at Gorge Days. I'll never forget the elation on the band's faces when Kenzie and I approached them after the concert when the well-dressed guy who had been talking to them had walked off.

They had kept their cool for all of two seconds. I smile, remembering how Ryder had lifted me and nearly crushed my ribs with the hug I'd received.

I still couldn't believe the whirlwind that had

happened after that. Studio time, practice, studio time again, promotional appearances on local radio stations. The first time I heard their song on the radio, I pulled over and screamed. I had such an intense sense of pride for these four individuals who had taught me so much about life and living over the summer.

God, I had missed them.

Every last one of them, especially one band member in particular.

My eyes lock with the tall, dark-haired guy dressed all in black who is standing beside a classic muscle car. In one of our many conversations about his parents, Ryder had mentioned how his dad had to sell a '69 Camaro because Ryder's mom had gotten pregnant with him and they'd needed the money to buy their first home. Ryder had said that one day he would buy the car back for his dad as a surprise.

There isn't a day that goes by that I don't ask Ryder about his parents. He called his dad when *The Frozen* had signed a recording contract and his dad had been genuinely happy for him, but his mom had managed to spoil the moment by telling him he needed to continue his education, because he would need his smarts to fall back on if the music thing failed.

I had always been brought up with the understanding that college was a necessity, especially in today's world, and I wanted to attend college...but I really wanted to go to Vancouver. I felt at home in Vancouver, and my friends were in Vancouver.

And Ryder was in Vancouver.

But now he is here, I think...and the closer I get to my boyfriend, the more nervous I become. His hair is even longer than when I'd left Vancouver, and my fingers are itching to dig into those waves.

Carl and I stop at the little security hut, where I sign out and Carl notes the time. He walks me toward Ryder, who meets us halfway.

"You kids be safe, alright?" Carl says.

Both Ryder and I reply, "We will."

Ryder's gaze shifts over me slowly. "I love the schoolgirl plaid. Makes me think of all the naughty things I can do to you."

I laugh nervously. Of course he liked the uniform. Most guys did.

He stares at me like I was his favorite flavor of ice cream. I will never get tired of that look.

"I dunno if I dare get into a car with you. I don't know what might happen."

"What are you afraid of?"

I swallow past the lump in my throat and look into his beautiful blue eyes. He's so gorgeous, he makes my heart hurt, and I'm reminded yet again of how much I have missed him. "I'm afraid that I might lose control."

He's on me in two seconds, pulling me close and giving me a long kiss. I melt into him as his hands move over my hips to my butt.

In the distance I hear girlish squeals. I can't help it. I smile against his lips.

I look over my shoulder and the girls from Sister Diane's physical education class are waving at us and cheering before the nun motions them into the building.

He flashes a devilish smile. "I told them I was your cousin, you know…so you'll have some explaining to do come Monday."

"I don't care what anyone thinks," I say, and I realize for the first time in my life I don't care. This is right. What I feel is right, and I don't question it.

"Come on," he says with a wink. "I have plans for us."

I get into the car and buckle myself in.

"How are you doing?" I ask, and he lifts my hand and places a kiss on my fingers. It's a sweet gesture, and one I feel all the way to my soul. Everything I've ever heard about

Joshua Ryder goes against the Joshua Ryder I know, the man who has told me his fears and his weaknesses. Maybe that's the difference. This is a different man—one who is a recovering addict who doesn't take his life for granted any longer. He's imperfect, and what I love most about him is that he's not afraid to poke fun at himself, or to admit his mistakes.

"My mom called me last night."

I lift my brows. "What did she say?"

"She wished me good luck on our trip and told me that she was proud of me."

He glances at me and grins. There is a light in his eyes I have never seen and it makes me smile.

"That was huge for me, you know? I don't think she's ever said those words to me before. She even said she wanted to see us perform."

"I'm happy for you," I say, squeezing his hand.

His fingers thread through mine. "We're going to get together for dinner when I return to Vancouver. I can't wait to see my brother."

"I bet he can't wait either." I was thrilled for Ryder, but I didn't want to be reminded of his leaving when he had only just arrived in San Diego.

He pulls into the parking lot of a well-known upscale hotel.

"Are you trying to impress me?" I ask as he pulls into a spot far away from the other cars.

"Is it working?" he asks, flashing that boyish smile that I love.

I would have been happy at a run-down motel. I just want to be with him. "Definitely."

There's a heavy-lidded look to his eyes that has me a little nervous and excited at the same time. "Where's Kenzie?" I blurt out.

"At the beach with Deklan, Brooke, and Curtis. Trust me, she wanted to come with me to pick you up, but I told her I wanted some time alone with you."

My heart starts racing.

"Are you afraid, Ange?" he asks, his voice husky as he opens my car door.

I step out and I look right at him. "No, not at all. I've been waiting for this moment for months."

Instead of a reply, I get lifted from the seat and then we're walking through the hotel lobby and into the elevator.

He pulls me against him and we're making out again.

By the time the elevator doors open, I'm flushed and more than a little turned on.

"I don't have to be back in L.A. until Monday, so I hope you can stay with me all weekend."

Oh, I would definitely be staying with him all weekend.

The room is standard posh—modern furnishings, medium size flat size television, and in the middle of the room was the king size bed.

My mouth goes dry. Ryder is looking at the bed as well.

The sun is shining through the windows, and I wish the sun would go down soon. I just never thought I'd lose my virginity in the light of day. I'd always imagined a candle-lit room with body friendly light instead of natural light that would no doubt enhance every feature I don't want my boyfriend to see the first time he sees me naked.

Oh my God…was I ready?

Oddly, as the seconds tick by any nervousness I thought I would feel dissipates.

His hands cup my face and he kisses me gently. "I want you, Ange. Do you feel what you do to me?" he asks, flexing his hips so I feel the hard ridge of his sex pressed against my belly.

"I want you, too."

Slowly he begins to undress me. He starts with the skirt, which is pooled at my feet. I kick it aside and take a second to slide my shoes off. His brows lift as he unbuttons my shirt and it immediately goes the way of my skirt. The only items remaining are my bra, panties, and socks.

He goes straight for the bra.

I am trembling with excitement and fear of the unknown.

Lifting me in his arms, he heads toward the bed, where we tumble onto the comforter. The second my back makes contact with the bed I lift his shirt up and over his head and toss it aside. I focus on his buckle and he laughs under his breath—a throaty chuckle that sends my desire to another level.

I'm surprised with how fast I have his pants unbuttoned and unzipped and am pushing them down his hips.

I think he is, too, because when he glances up at me he looks ready to devour me.

I'll never forget that look in a million years, or the sensations rushing through me.

"I want you," I repeat the words I said minutes ago.

He replies with a kiss that has my blood simmering in my veins. My fingers are running over the hard planes of his back and resting on the ridge of his briefs.

This is the point of no return.

I pull his underwear down and he does the rest.

He feels me through my panties, his hands sliding over the silk, and then he's pulling them down my thighs and legs and tossing them aside. He goes up on his knees and pulls off my stockings one at a time, kissing the insides of my thighs before he flings the stockings onto the floor.

My eyes wander over his athletic body, coming to rest on his cock. I swallow hard as I stare, and I am stunned at my own brazenness when I reach for him, testing the feel of him in my hand as I slide my fingers from the base of his shaft up toward the head. The skin is velvety soft—and in such contrast to the rock hard phallus that twitches in response to my touch.

Ryder groans and I smile, amazed at the power I have over him at this moment. My fingers curl around him and just when I find a certain rhythm, he pushes my hand away, and I'm once again on my back and he is kissing the insides of my thighs.

"Relax," he says with a grin, and I do as he asks, but it's nearly impossible when my most private of places is three inches from his face.

His gaze shifts to my sex, and then his face is there.

My breath catches in my throat as his tongue strokes my slit and teases the tiny bundle of nerves at the top of my sex.

My hands grip the comforter at my sides, and I'm doing everything I can to not lift my hips against his mouth.

I fail miserably. Soon I'm fisting his hair and calling out his name, and saying other things I never thought would pass my lips.

I have no control and he loves it, his low, throaty groan turning me on even more.

My stomach tightens and I feel as tightly pulled as a bowstring as he continues to tease my clit with tiny strokes of his tongue.

"Ryder?"

Ryder

She calls out my name and it's both a question and an exclamation.

Her climax comes fast and strong, and I'm amazed as I watch her ride out the new sensations.

When she opens her eyes, her mouth is open and she's panting. The sides of her mouth lift slowly and she reaches for me.

All my plans to stretch this out and savor every second mock me, because all I want to do is bury myself deep inside her. I reach into the side table and pull out a rubber. She told me she had her sister take her to the clinic so she could be on the pill, but it's only been a few weeks, and I would never take that chance.

I slide the rubber on and look at her. There is no fear in her eyes. Just desire.

We kiss, and I slow it down, telling myself to calm down.

Control, I say to myself as I slide between her thighs.

"I want you," she says, and the intensity in her face takes my need to a whole different level.

I ease into her heat.

She sucks in a breath.

I immediately come upon resistance. I'd never had a virgin before, and I'm touched that she's waited for me.

I kiss her softly at the same time I thrust.

She stiffens at the intrusion and stops kissing me back. But only for a second. She shifts slightly, adjusting, and lifts her hips.

I slowly begin to move.

Soon she is moving along with me, kissing my neck, my shoulder, her fingernails biting into the skin of my shoulders as she gets closer to orgasm. I pull out nearly all the way, and slowly enter again.

"Oh my God," she whispers.

I love her sounds—the groans, the moans, the dirty words and way she says my name. I'll never get enough of her…ever.

Again I slowly slide out. She won't have it. She grabs my ass with both hands and pulls me close.

I follow with shorter thrusts that have her panting. Her hips meet mine, thrust for thrust, and soon I've hit the point of no return.

Her eyes are closed tight.

"Open your eyes, Ange," I whisper against her lips.

Immediately she does as I ask.

I'll never forget the look in those eyes for as long as I live. As I thrust, her breath catches in her throat, and she cries out as her inner muscles pull me in further and deeper. Her climax is so strong that it sends me over the edge, and I am a man possessed. A few more thrusts and I'm finding my own release and falling into the arms of the woman I love.

For long minutes I lay on her, trying to catch my breath. She's playing with my hair with one hand, the other brushing along my spine.

I have never known such contentment and peace.

Everything in my life is perfect.

I have the life I want, the career I want, the best friend a guy can ask for, and a woman who has made me feel more loved in the short time that I've known her than all the woman I've known combined. She makes me believe I can do anything.

I lift my head and stare into her beautiful eyes.

She grins. "Wow, now I get it."

I roll off her and bring her with me. I go up on an elbow. "What to you get?"

She laughs softly. "The Ryder Affect."

I laugh and kiss her.

"You've ruined me for all other men. I hope you know that."

I know she says the words teasingly, but I take them seriously. The thought of Ange with anyone else makes me angry. I would never give her a reason to walk away.

"Hey," she says, her brows furrowing in that way I loved. "Why are you frowning?"

I slide my fingers through hers. "You're *my* girl, Ange. Mine."

"You sound so territorial."

"I *am* territorial. I mean it…you're mine. I know that we'll have physical distance between us with you living in San Diego and me in Vancouver, but I swear I'll be the man you deserve."

Her gaze shifts from mine and drops down to my body. Her lips curve slightly as she pushes me onto my back and rolls on top of me. "And I'll be the woman you deserve."

I push the waterfall of reddish-brown curls back from her face. "You already are."

ABOUT J.A. TEMPLETON

J.A. Templeton is the YA/New Adult pen name for romance author Julia Templeton. The author of over twenty novels, Julia enjoys reading, research, traveling, riding motorcycles, and spending time with family and friends. A certified psychic medium, Julia is married to her high school sweetheart, has two grown children, and four grandchildren. She lives in the beautiful Pacific Northwest and loves hearing from readers.

Stay connected with J.A.

J.A.'s website:
http://www.jatempleton.com

J.A.'s Twitter:
https://twitter.com/JATempleton

J.A.'s Facebook:
https://www.facebook.com/pages/JA-Temple-ton/124655067647202?ref=hl

www.ingramcontent.com/pod-product-compliance
Lightning Source LLC
Chambersburg PA
CBHW060149130626
46556CB00006B/2560